Just Ducky

LaVerne St. George

Table of Contents

COPYRIGHT

Just Ducky ©2025 by LaVerne St. George

All Rights Reserved
Electronic Edition
ISBN: 978-0-9969778-5-2
Print Edition
ISBN: 978-0-9969778-6-9

 Open Book Romances
www.openbookromances.com
An Imprint of Open Book Communications
Durham, NC

Cover design by LaVerne St. George

DEDICATION

To the doctors, scientists, humanitarian healthcare workers, and public health officials all over the world who work tirelessly to monitor animals and humans for new influenza virus strains that may cause a pandemic... and have.

ACKNOWLEDGEMENTS

No matter the solitary hours of typing, or putting pen to paper, editing or planning, no book is written alone. My sincere thanks goes to my First Readers for JUST DUCKY! — Suzi Holler, Julie Evanchek, Pamela Schaepe, Rick Ellrod, Joyce Sykes, and Steph Dawning. Susan, Mara, Seralynn, and Matto of the Durham Romance Writer Friends always provide solid feedback and helped me strengthen my portrayals of Marian and Gill. Thanks to Lesley Looper, Head of the Shelf Preparation Section at Duke University Libraries, who helped me put Marian and her technical services job into perspective.

Finally, a thank you must be sent to the producers, directors, and crew of the Netflix documentary series PANDEMIC: HOW TO PREVENT AN OUTBREAK, with special appreciation for the doctors, scientists, humanitarian healthcare workers, and public health officials profiled in the series. Released on January 22, 2020, this eerily timed, six-part documentary covers a variety of issues and circumstances from which a new respiratory virus might arise and recommendations for prevention. By March 2020, the United States was fighting such a virus: COVID-19. Episode 3, "Seek, Don't Hide," documents the duck sampling performed regularly to monitor viral genetics. This episode became my inspiration for JUST DUCKY! and the setting of an important moment for Marian and Gill.

CHAPTER ONE

The Past Says Hello

Outside a car door slammed. Voices drifted up through the second-floor window. Decidedly male.

Marian Fletcher rolled her shoulders and shoved the sounds from her attention. With blunt tweezers, she picked up the diamond-shaped, brightly colored postage stamp and slipped it into a pre-cut plastic mount. After lightly brushing the mount's adhesive back across a damp sponge, Marian glued the mount with its stamp on to a large, pre-printed album page headed "PORTUGUESE GUINEA." A full-colored, accurate illustration of an African egg-eating snake—in the process of devouring a large egg—glowed from under the clear plastic.

Looks good, Marian. You've done that exactly right.

Her dad's voice rose from her memory and made her smile. She had just turned twelve and with her father, had been mounting stamps for an exhibit on storks. She could almost feel his hand on her shoulder. His encouragement. They had never finished the exhibit. Four months later, her dad had been gone, killed by a drunk driver while changing a tire for a stranded tourist out on Coastal Highway 17. She laid a hand over the album page in honor and in gratitude.

Outside, another car door slammed. More voices. Female and male. Laughter.

Marian shook off the bittersweet memories. She swiped the screen of her laptop and used the electronic stamp manager to verify the Scott Catalog number and type in the date acquired—last Saturday at a stamp show in downtown Wilmington.

The rumble of a truck caught her attention and grew louder as it approached. The unmistakable thunk and groan of a disengaged lock and a heavy metal accordion door sliding open filled the air. From the noise, it seemed the moving crew next door was getting an early start.

Curiosity pushed Marian out of her office chair. In a few steps, she reached the window overlooking the front yard and saw... chaos. No, she amended. Controlled chaos. A steady line of people toting boxes and small furniture moved like a determined ant army through the jumble of kitchen chairs, floor lamps, and rugs scattered across the grass, up the walk, up the three steps, and into the door of townhouse B, the home adjoining Marian's own townhouse A. In a short time, the people-ants retraced their steps to collect more items from the hands of two men unloading.

So, the new tenant had arrived, just as her landlord, Mrs. Fossey, had said.

"He's a professor over at UNC Wilmington. Works on something to do with the flu. Nice man. About your age. Good-looking, too, I must say." Elinor Fossey had added that last comment with a twinkle in her eye and a sly smile that told Marian the older woman must have had her share of admirers back in the day. "He's taking over for one of the biology faculty who had a heart attack."

Dr. Abrams. Marian sent up a quick prayer for the professor's recovery, and another for herself. Dr. Abrams had been her partner in a project that Marian had agreed to as part of her five-year plan. She hoped to move from cataloging, a position that worked away from the public, and into reference services where she could interact directly with students and faculty. The current Sciences Librarian planned to retire in the next year or two, and Marian was determined to apply for his position. She had a strong science background and knew the library's collections, but she needed the project with Dr. Abrams to demonstrate her ability to work with faculty. Dr. Abrams' illness meant waiting for a replacement from the Biology and Marine Biology department, and Marian chafed at the delay.

"Gill! We can start unpacking if you tell us where you want things."

At the call from the porch, Marian's attention focused. One of the men trotted down the truck's ramp to join a woman in the middle of the yard.

Gill. Her new neighbor. He *was* good-looking. He had the build of a tennis player—medium height, all lean muscle nicely outlined by blue jeans and a navy UNCW sweatshirt emblazoned with the Seahawks logo. He had a great smile which came easily as he talked with the dark-haired woman. His brown hair avoided being completely ordinary due to its thickness and slight wave. The eastern half of North Carolina was having a mid-February cold snap, and puffs of air became visible as the two talked. Something about his stance tugged at her.

She stared. Shook her head. *No, it can't be.*

Then he laughed, a simple outburst of joy, and memory rushed through her. Marian swung from the window and clasped her hands together. Burton Gillespie, star tennis player at New Hanover High. The focus of a crush that had lasted much of her senior year.

Marian straightened her shoulders. He had been one of the popular set; she had not. She had experienced both pleasure and heartache in the fantasy and longing.

She crossed her arms. In any case, it had all been such a long time ago. Twelve years, in fact. She was an adult now, not a teenager. She might agree with Mrs. Fossey on the man and admire the moving operation's organization, but she had the other five stamps of the Portuguese Guinea set to mount.

About thirty minutes later, she had reached stamp number four when the doorbell rang. She descended the staircase, opened the door... and blinked.

"Hi. Gill Gillespie, your new neighbor." He held out his hand. Through a fog of conflicting emotions, she took it, knew she was staring but couldn't stop. His brow furrowed. "We'll be sharing a wall?"

Marian found her voice. "Yes, of course. I saw. I can see that." Her hand flicked toward the yard. She cleared her throat. "But I know you, right? Burton?" She hoped against hope he'd deny it.

His eyes widened at the name. His lips quirked. "I go by Gill now." He studied her for a moment longer, and Marian thought she would not be surprised if he had no memory of her.

Then his expression cleared. "Marian? Marian Fletcher. Of course. We had English together."

His eyes swept over her. She knew what he saw. Something not much removed from her high school days. Shoulder-length mouse-brown hair, bangs and ends cut razor-straight. Brown eyes with no touch of anything so flattering as a golden highlight behind glasses with dark blue frames. No makeup over pale skin. Her pea-green, long-sleeved cotton shirt, neatly pressed, over tan linen slacks. Brown ballerina slides.

She nodded. "Mr. Cameron."

Gill nodded and grinned. "Cameron. Yeah. A stickler for dangling participles."

She felt an answering smile tug at her lips and fought it. "He was, yes."

Gill shifted. "You look good."

Now her smile won. "Thanks. You, too." Awkward silence hovered. Marian sighed inwardly. He had been part of the party crowd. Still seemed to be a crowd kind of guy. She had been closer to wallpaper. Preferred it even now. No reason to be any more connected twelve years later.

"So, what can I do for you?" she asked.

Relief flushed across his face. "Right. Do you have a Phillips screwdriver I could borrow? Mine's at the bottom of a box."

"Sure, let me get it." Her manners kicked in. "Please, come in and close the door. It's pretty cold today."

"Sure is."

The words trailed after her, and she heard the click of the front door as she walked into the garage and pulled the toolbox out of the metal cupboard. As she returned, she watched him looking around but standing right where she had left him.

He had manners. She'd give him that.

When she handed the box to him, he asked, "You sure you want me to take the whole thing?"

"Yes. Use what you need. Just leave it on the porch when you're finished."

"Thanks a lot. I will." With a wave, he opened the door and walked back across the lawn.

Marian stood with her hand holding the edge of the door and watched him stride away as if he needed to be somewhere to do something important. He had always been that way. He had moved through the halls of New Hanover High, the dining hall, across the tennis courts as if he were on a mission. Always surrounded by friends, girls.

Marian bit her lip. And here he was, living next door. Professor, Mrs. Fossey had said, at UNCW. She sighed. She might be able to avoid him at work. Mrs. Fossey had mentioned the flu and biology, but even though Marian's specialty was science, she worked in cataloging. So probably not. But the campus wasn't huge, so there was a chance of running into him. It might not be so bad, she thought as she closed the door and locked it.

In high school, he had looked terrific in tennis whites.

Marian shook off the memory and climbed the stairs, settled back at her worktable, and got busy mounting the last of the snake set.

A bump vibrated against the wall to her left. Muted voices wafted into her workroom. More bumps, shouts, laughter. Marian pushed back from her chair and looked out the window. The boxes had vanished, and larger furniture dotted the lawn., the ant-like procession had altered into the precision movement of each piece by one or more friends, depending on the piece's size.

The snakes now safe under plastic, Marian pulled her stock box off the shelf in front of her and pulled out a glassine envelope. A set of twelve ducks from Antigua. This is what she'd really been after on her weekend trip to the stamp auction. Ducks. Ever since her father first took her on outings to the local parks and marshes, she had always been fascinated by these birds who could swim and fly with equal skill. There were even a few duck families that lived in the large pond beyond the low trees behind her duplex. When she had found stamps illustrating different species, she had gotten hooked.

She pulled out her collection book and slipped the glassine envelope into one of the slots on the book's light cardboard pages. She had almost every occurrence of a duck depicted on a stamp worldwide, and she thought this might be an exhibit that could win her a medal at the Southeastern Stamp Expo next January. She had wanted to win for a long time. In memory of her father. She brushed her fingers over the page, missing him, the one in the family most like her.

The exhibit didn't have a theme yet. Just having all the duck stamps didn't mean an award-winning exhibit. She needed something interesting to draw the stamps and the outside world together. Perhaps a bit of research on why each country chose ducks—

Music blared through the wall.

Marian jumped. Under her fingers, the stock book slid across the table and dropped to the floor. Wailing guitar, insistent beat, throaty vocals, singer... unfamiliar. Rock. Not classic rock. Definitely not classic.

Her heart lodged in her throat, Marian stooped down to pick up the stock book and inspected the stamps and envelopes inside for any creases or damage that might decrease their value. She didn't draw a full breath again until the stock book lay tucked in a drawer.

Hands on hips, she stood glaring at the wall, her mind running options. Option One. Pound on the wall, stomp to his door, and demand he kill the music. Option Two. Dial up her own music, maybe something classical, like the big, bold *1812 Overture*. A battery of cannons blasting away might do the trick.

Then she took a deep breath. Those were the options her mother and sister always chose. And she had worked too long and too hard to avoid becoming either of those two women, even though she loved them dearly.

She decided on Option One, without the pounding, stomping and the demand. Just a simple request from a neighbor. Polite. With a smile.

Nodding sharply, pleased with her decision, Marian started to the door.

The music stopped. The silence vibrated for long seconds, and Marian felt every muscle in her body relax. No confrontation, no conversation needed, it seemed.

"Thank you, God." She didn't talk to God much, but she did know when to show gratitude. Especially after being rescued from a face-to-face with Burton. No, Gill.

A second after that whispered prayer, the music—same channel—floated through the walls again, but much softer.

She could live with that.

Seemed Burton... Gill. She couldn't seem to make that switch, although she had to admit she liked that he had changed it. *Gill* may have changed his name but not his character. Still the party guy, surrounded by friends, right in the middle of wherever the action was. Tennis whites or not, he was not going to be the ideal neighbor.

She sighed.

Her former neighbors had been an elderly couple, content to watch reruns of *The Andy Griffith Show* or sit on the porch swing during the soft, southern evenings. Quietly.

She was going to miss them.

CHAPTER TWO

The Duck Connection

Gill Gillespie threaded his way through the rugs, sofa, and the chairs on the lawn, the heavy toolbox in his hand—what on earth did she have in this thing? — and hopped up the porch stairs.

Marian Fletcher. He remembered her from high school. Super smart, really quiet, loved anything written by Edgar Allen Poe. She hadn't changed much. Haircut still the same. Although it had a pretty kind of shine to it. And her brown eyes were dwarfed by the oversized blue frames.

Something in those eyes judged him. Found him lacking. Well, no surprise there. Plenty of people did. His parents. His sister Claire. Susan. Gretchen. Tina. Almost every girl he'd ever dated seriously.

Except Natalie, a good friend. The best, really.

In the living room, he set the toolbox beside the coffee table, the one with the shaky leg. Then he opened the lid and stared in amazement.

Brent Carver, a friend from college and a faculty member in the UNCW History department, whistled. "Will you look at that? That's the neatest toolbox I've ever seen."

"Organized to the max." Every tool was placed in a perfectly sized space for it. When he pulled off the top insert, the small plastic boxes underneath were filled with screws, bolts, and nails of different sizes, each size having its own place. The living room he had glimpsed from the entryway had hinted at her tidiness, and he considered himself an orderly guy, as guys went, but this—

"I'll say. Wish my hardware store was as organized. Got to hire this guy to organize my space."

"Girl."

"What?"

"The uber-organizer is a woman. Someone I went to high school with if you can believe that."

"Still. The woman has some skills. She good-looking?"

Gill thought a moment, remembering her unstylish clothes, but also remembering her shining hair and clear skin. "Not bad. Probably would want to organize the heck out of a guy's life, though."

"Too true."

"Hey Brent!" A female voice called from upstairs. "Come up here and help with the bedframe."

"On my way," he called, then added to Gill, "If we don't break the bedframe, you just might have a place to sleep tonight."

"Works for me."

Gill tightened the screws under the table and tested its stability. Satisfied, he shifted on his knees to replace the screwdriver, and his hand hovered for a moment while he examined the box. No toolbox should be that neat. There must be a rule written somewhere about that. He had an urge to jumble everything up, so it wouldn't look so perfect, so tidy. Then he thought again of the tidy, buttoned-down woman who was now his neighbor. If he ever wanted to drive her crazy, he knew how he could do it. He grinned wickedly. Might come in handy someday. He placed the screwdriver back into its slot.

As work proceeded in his new home, he answered endless questions about where things should go, set people to work unpacking boxes, and made sure the right stuff got into the right room. Thinking of Marian, he decided not to worry about where everything ended up. He'd find it later. All he needed for the next couple of days was packed in two boxes marked "Personal."

Then someone suggested music, and the heavy rock nearly deafened him. The roar continued, accompanied by laughter, but Gill could almost see Marian glaring at the wall that separated the two townhomes. He had better do something or she'd be over here, bringing her judging eyes with her.

Then someone shouted, "Turn that down! Can't hear myself think!" The music volume dropped.

Gill let out a breath. Crisis averted.

The long moving day progressed through unpacking, a dinner break of pizza and cold drinks, and more unpacking until Brent was the last one out, loading broken-down moving boxes into the rental truck and waving good-bye as he drove off.

Then there was silence.

Blessed silence.

Gill opened the door that led from the kitchen to the back deck set a few inches off the ground and viewed the swath of grass in the fading light, the moon already bright and high overhead. The light breeze felt cool on his skin. He sipped from his glass of tea that someone—Marcie, maybe?—had brought. The sweetness made his teeth ache, and he saluted the tea-maker with his glass. At graduate school in Maryland, he hadn't been able to get a decent glass of iced tea. A prayer of thanks rose effortlessly, and he spoke softly into the night.

"You must be working overtime for me, God. I do appreciate it. I'm in the right place at the right time to finish my research and get a publication out before the end of the year. After two years back in Wilmington, I've got this great house within walking distance of UNCW."

He took another sip of tea.

"My family still expects me to be part of the whole society scene, country club, social events, Mother's parties. You and I have had this conversation before, and I know I have to continue to let them know that's not who I am anymore. With your help, I'll do it.

"Thanks for new UNCW friends and a safe move-in. Thanks for a new neighbor, who at the very least will be quiet. And you know how I need my downtime. Which reminds me. Gotta return the toolbox. And I have a great view of the rising moon."

He took another drink, then saluted the heavens with the glass. "Thanks."

***

Gill wondered how thankful he should be as he sat in Emilio Salazar's office on Monday afternoon, listening in some dismay to the department chairman's proposal.

"It's one of those ideas coming from the Dean's office. An opportunity to show off the good working relationships between departments on campus. Shows how we get great things done when we work together. And it's important that these exhibits make some connection to the city of Wilmington."

"To Wilmington?"

"Yes, yes. The Dean wants to highlight how our faculty are an integral part of the city's life."

Gill wondered if frequenting local pizzerias or using the tennis courts could count as being an "integral part" of the city.

Salazar continued. "Now, Biology and Marine Biology was all set with Dr. Abrams working with the Randall Library but of course he's not able to continue, and from what I understand, he and his partner—can't remember the name at the moment—were well on their way."

"I'm not sure I'll have time," Gill protested. "I'm trying to get my lab set up."

But the man was off and running. He was of medium build and shimmering with energy. Brent had warned him to beware. When Dr. Salazar was on a mission, nothing short of a nuclear explosion could stop him.

"Everyone says they don't have enough time, but I can't imagine that picking up Dr. Abrams's classes would be all that challenging since you have his course outlines. Right? And I think it would be pretty simple to step in when Dr. Abrams has already made the connection."

I could use a nuclear warhead right now. Gill gave him a nod.

"I do remember you telling me at your interview that you were looking forward to having a tenure-track position here and a solid opportunity for your academic future. Tenure has a lot to do with publications..." *Understatement,* Gill thought. "...but it also has to do with contributing to the university and its mission in a tangible way."

Yes, I do want tenure. The stability, the honor. Hadn't realized Dr. Salazar's interpretation of "contributing" might be a little broad.

Well then. Setting up his lab was going to take a lot longer than he had planned.

Which had led to him walking into Randall Library on Tuesday and asking to see the librarian who had been working with Dr. Abrams.

With a sinking feeling, he watched her walk toward him. The brown skirt topped by a bright yellow blouse and tan sweater combination did nothing for her complexion.

"Marian." He held out his hand, hoping to hide his reaction to the dreadful colors behind the social manners drummed into him since boyhood. "Good to see you."

The polite smile pasted on her face told him how she felt about this meeting.

She took his hand. "Good to see you, too."

Two things happened at once. Gill realized that she had caught his negative reaction, which touched off a flash of embarrassment inside him, and he felt the grip of her hand, warm and smooth under his, conveying her professionalism in her touch. The combination set him off balance for a moment. Then he withdrew his hand and soldiered on with the niceties.

"By the way, thanks for the toolbox. It came in handy. I left it on your porch on Sunday morning. You weren't home."

"Thank you. I was at church. I saw it when I got back." Something about the way she said the words raised the hair on the back of his neck. As if everyone ought to be at church on Sunday. He was going to point out that he actually had been in church early on Sunday, but another impression hit him.

She didn't seem to like him for some reason. He rolled that through his mind.

On the other hand, she didn't linger or indicate she meant anything by it. Maybe he was too sensitive.

"So, this project with Dr. Abrams you were working on..."

She motioned toward a hall. "Let's talk in my office. Did you speak with Dr. Abrams or Dr. Salazar? Get any background?"

"Dr. Salazar. Some background. He spent a lot of time pointing out that it would be to my advantage to get with the plan." After that last came out, Gill wondered if he should apologize. She might think he didn't want to work with her. If she had taken a dislike to him, maybe he didn't.

Surprisingly, she gave a short laugh. "That does sound like him. I'd advise staying out of his way when he's stirring up things. It's all too easy to get sucked into the vortex."

"You're the second person who has warned me of his tendencies. He hooked me this time, but I've got to admit, he was trying to be helpful."

"I wouldn't doubt it. He's very supportive of his faculty. At any rate, the point of the exhibit—exhibits, really, because the library will host a set of presentations here—is to show the collaborations between different departments on campus. Dr. Abrams's research focused on swine diseases, so we had decided to create an exhibit for one of the cases that would describe his research and point out what resources in the library support his efforts."

"Including you."

Both her voice and her walking paused. Gill wasn't sure why that had popped out, except that he objected to the way she had said "resources" as if it were only databases, books, and journals that were important. He knew he would have never made it through his Ph.D. program without the research librarians.

"Including me." The words held a touch of revelation, as if she and others didn't often acknowledge the role the profession played in the world of research.

She took a few more steps and opened a door into her office.

As he might have guessed, there was order here. Books in neat rows in a tall bookcase. A bookcart packed with books, paper slips visible from the tops. A large computer monitor screen saver drifting through a standard collage of colorful blocks. A chair and desk that you might see in any modern office, a stack of papers set precisely to one side. She gestured to the extra chair, and they both sat.

"Well, I'm into ducks, not swine, so—" Gill began.

"Ducks." She interrupted so quietly that Gill wondered if he had misheard. He leaned in. "Ducks," she repeated in a more normal tone. "Your research concerns ducks?"

She was studying his face with an expression that held a touch of awe in it. He wondered if he should wipe his face.

Then he found himself staring. She had the most wonderful eyes. Milk chocolate brown, wide and clear. Even the large eyeglass frames and lenses couldn't hide them. The silence stretched.

Gill swallowed and found his voice. "Yes. And how ducks might help us avert an influenza pandemic."

"Ducks might? How?"

He sat back, giving himself a few seconds before explaining. "The Influenza A virus caused the flu pandemic of 1918 as well as the ones in 1968 and 2009, so the Centers for Disease Control and the science community are always monitoring viral genetic material. We know there are three genetic subtypes, and each subtype originated from a different species. Pigs, humans, and birds, specifically water fowl like swans, geese, and ducks. We also know that pigs and humans can carry two subtypes at the same time, but birds are like super-carriers because they can carry all three subtypes at the same time. Are you with me so far?"

This was about the place in his explanation when he would see a glazed look or a patient smile from his listener. Instead, Marian's smile had grown, and those brown eyes sparkled as if backlit by small flames. *Pretty.* "Yes. Absolutely."

"The viral genetic material, the RNA, from the subtypes can intermix and recombine with each other. Most of the time, this mixing just makes more virus that we've seen before, so either people have immunity already or our vaccines can take care of it quickly. In some rare instances –like in 1918, 1968 and 2009—a new mix was created, and humans had no immunity to the new mix. By the time vaccines could be developed, millions worldwide had died. Birds are the key."

Marian nodded. "Because they can carry all three subtypes and provide more chances for a rare mix to occur."

"Exactly." Gill felt his excitement rising as it always did when talking about his research. Especially with someone who seemed as interested as Marian. "And migrating ducks are good subjects for sampling. Large flocks fly and rest together. Easy to gather and sample. In North Carolina, we sample teal and wood duck populations. We're quite certain that studying the viral RNA that ducks carry will help us determine when the next flu pandemic will rise in humans. If we start to find brand new combined strands of RNA in the ducks, we could sound an early alarm. Ducks can give us the clue."

"That's... wonderful." Marian grinned, and Gill found himself smiling back as she continued. "I'm a huge fan of ducks. My father and I used to feed the ducks at the park near our house." Her smile dimmed. She seemed to realize her personal sharing was out of character. Or maybe unprofessional. She lowered her head and cleared her throat before meeting his gaze again.

"I have an idea," she continued, her voice rising in tone. "We have to show our connection with the community, right?" Gill nodded, mystified yet hopeful he might be off the hook for that part. "What do you think about stamps?"

His brain stumbled over the question as a sudden thought appeared. *Man, I'll never call her eyes "plain brown." Not ever again.*

He forced himself to refocus on the question. "Stamps? I'm for them. For the mail. In general."

She tilted her head, and her lips quirked. "Good. That's... good. If you're willing to meet at my house, I can show you what I have in mind for the humble postage stamp."

"Influenza A. Ducks. Stamps. I'm not sure I get it."

"A stretch, I know, and you may think the whole idea is crazy. But take a look first. It'd be better if I showed you. Then decide. All right?"

Her face had flushed pink, and she sat still in the chair. Waiting. The energy of her eagerness brushed across him and tugged at him. Flu, ducks, and stamps. Since he didn't have a better idea...

"All right." She glowed. Gill's mind went blank for a moment. He brought himself back to the matter at hand. "When?"

They agreed upon a meeting time on Thursday to "take a look" and plan the exhibit, whatever they decided about her stamp idea. Gill walked across campus toward his office, his mind whirling.

It seems the uber-organizer collects stamps. Fits perfectly. And ducks. She likes ducks. Gill whistled softly. *Who'd have thought Marian Fletcher would like fluffy, quacking, wet, disorderly ducks?*

He smiled.

Well if ducks make her eyes shine like that, bring on the stamps!

CHAPTER THREE

The Ducks Have It

Gill set down his phone.

Thank God I had my coffee before Mother called.

When it came to her events, the woman was relentless. The fundraiser was more than a month away, and she was already twisting his arm to attend and beg... that was, ask politely and firmly for donations.

A fundraiser for the aquarium at Ft. Fisher. That I can probably do.

He finished his breakfast of now-soggy sugar-coated flakes and milk. His mother probably had his class schedule noted in her planner, he decided, because she always seemed to call on his mornings off.

Except this wasn't really a morning off. It was Thursday, and he had that meeting with Marian at ten. He checked his watch. Still time. Over more coffee he reviewed Dr. Abrams's notes, and while he was adding his own notations, a modern country song began on his phone. He noted the name, debated whether to answer, and gave in.

"Good morning, Claire."

"Are you going to Russell's wedding?"

That was his sister. Right to the point. "When is it?"

"Second Saturday in March."

"That's three weeks away, Claire. I don't know." He reminded himself to be patient. She was family.

"You have to go. Mother and Dad have another engagement. Some company event. If I have to go, you have to go. Put it on your calendar."

"Claire—"

"I'll see you and Natalie there."

"I'm not bringing—" The connection broke. "Natalie."

Gill stared at the phone. Rolled his shoulders. Neither woman took No for an answer.

Lord, how do I say No when they hang up? He shook off the frustration. No matter, he had weeks to decide. He glanced at the clock. 9:55. And a meeting right now.

He slipped everything into his leather messenger bag along with his tablet and notebook. All he had to do was walk next door and knock. He could get used to this kind of schedule.

Marian opened the door, and Gill found himself faced with another plain outfit—brown slacks and navy tee with a lightweight off-white jacket shot through with diagonal navy pinstripes. Neat and professional.

"Let's head upstairs. I'll show you what I'm thinking."

She led the way down a short hall past the kitchen and through the living room on the right to a staircase.

An old-fashioned word came to Gill. Immaculate. Everything in its place. He saw some pictures of people, perhaps family, on the end tables. No distinctive artwork, but seascapes and paintings of dunes sporting waving sea oats you might find in the galleries in Wrightsville Beach. In the pictures, he could see a hint of her love for the ocean and in the upright piano standing against one wall, a possible musical skill, but the traditional décor gave him nothing else. Not that he was interested, he told himself. He was just curious. Trying to determine where her reaction to him on Tuesday had come from. Before the ducks came up. He couldn't imagine what he'd done wrong to earn her dislike. He shrugged mentally. Nothing. He had done nothing. He'd just have to move on.

As he climbed the stairs to an open balcony above the living room, Gill decided he was looking forward to this exhibit project. The stamp idea had intrigued him because it was different from the dry text-and-graph posters that usually described scientific research. He was all for anything that would draw the eye and lighten up the presentation, engaging students and faculty alike. He and Marian had been on the same page there.

Then she made a quick left and opened a door into a room at the front of the townhouse.

Gill entered and stopped. The scene was so... unexpected.

On the walls hung colorful posters from the U.S. Postal Service depicting stamps—the new issue for Star Trek, a stunning set for women in science.

Smaller frames protected several scenes of ducks, all fashioned from colored yarns and remarkably life-like. Mallards, green-winged teals, wood ducks, and ruddy ducks were depicted swimming in ponds, nesting, playing in the tall reeds. He wondered who had the skill with the needle, Marian or someone else.

No doubt this was a workroom. And a retreat. Here was the reflection of Marian's personality under the organization. And there was organization in spades.

A grid of cubbyholes covered the short wall to the right. The plastic boxes in each hole could slide out to reveal their treasures.

Because they, no doubt, held treasures to this woman. Like his sister who crafted beaded jewelry which had earned praise at regional jewelry shows. Similar layout. Similar care. Bookshelves beside the window on the opposite wall carried oversized albums like hefty scrapbooks, three or four inches thick, protected by sturdy covers in dark colors. Each album was meticulously labelled, standing like a soldier ready for its next assignment.

On the work table, Marian had laid out heavy pages lined with rows of paperboard slots which held either opaque envelopes or small pieces of paper, some with delicate scalloped edges, others straight and sharp.

"I belong to the Stamp Club here in Wilmington, and I know the group would be delighted to have stamp collecting highlighted in the exhibit. I thought we could use the stamps as illustrations of the ducks that are integral to your research. Set up the exhibit like a stamp exhibit. Add pages to describe your research, and other items to show how the library supports your work. Are you with me so far?"

At that, Gill's attention moved from the rows of stamps to her face. "I'm with you."

"So here's what I have for the green-winged teal and blue-winged teal that you mentioned as part of your research, and here are the wood ducks, and the other local species that have been previously tagged and tested for Influenza A in North Carolina."

She pointed to each set. The United States, Ghana, Nicaragua, Australia. Not only beautiful and artistic renderings of biology and nature, but also a geography lesson and a window on the importance of ducks in countries who chose to honor these winged sources of food, pleasure and research on postage stamps that nearly everyone would see. He leaned down, peering intently. A pair of long tweezers appeared in his vision.

"If you want to look at any of them, just use these to lift them out." He wasn't sure he trusted himself to handle these carefully stored, fragile items, but then she had handed him the tweezers. The way she held the tool, he could see tension in her fingers. A little wary, he decided, but determined.

He pulled out several stamps one by one and then gingerly put them back. His mind began working on how to interweave a narrative about his research with these illustrations.

"I had another idea." She cleared her throat, and he straightened.

She jerked back to avoid being knocked in the chin by his abrupt movement, and he retreated a step. Gill exchanged a look of sheepish apology with Marian and gestured for her to continue.

"There are some stamps that are related to the World Health Organization. Do you work with the WHO?"

"I haven't directly. Anything on the National Institutes of Health?"

"No. Nothing on the Centers for Disease Control either. But there are some U.S. stamps depicting health research."

Gill thought a moment. "Pull those out and the ones about the WHO. The WHO is a great angle to bring into the presentation. We're talking about the threat of worldwide pandemic, so bringing in the WHO would remind readers what we do here reaches beyond the U.S. Can change the course of a disease and medicine across the globe."

Marian clasped her hands together. "Good. That's good."

And she glowed. From her smile to a slight flush in her cheeks to that back-light effect in her eyes. It seemed stamps did have the same effect as ducks. Pretty darn amazing. He drew a breath.

"So how do we do this?"

Now she moved easily to draw one of the albums off the shelf. After twisting off the screw tops of the three posts holding the pages in, she pulled out four letter-sized pages and laid them out. "This is how stamps are displayed for exhibit."

He saw that the stamps were mounted, like the miniature artwork they were, under protective plastic and near each stamp or grouping was a description of the topic, why the stamps were issued, and interesting facts. In this case the topic was women scientists, a postage-stamp version, literally, of the pictures on the poster.

"So the theme for this exhibit would be to focus on the local ducks' relation to the influenza research? Like the spring capture and testing for new viral combinations?"

"Yes, the ducks will introduce the subject. We can add how fall and winter duck hunting contribute to the effort when hunters allow the research team to test their kills. Brings in the connection to local hunters."

"And you know about the winter research... how?"

There was that frown again, and Gill tensed at the disapproval. "I'm a librarian, Dr. Gillespie. I look up things. I ask questions. I read."

He blushed. "Sorry. That's not what I meant. It came out wrong. I meant you've pulled this all together since Tuesday. This couldn't have been part of Dr. Abrams's project."

"No, of course not. Since we don't have much time until the presentation at the end of March, I thought I'd better get started right away. And I wanted to have something to show you today. Luckily, I was able to find a few articles about previous duck captures and testing in North Carolina and a bit more about influenza. It's pretty fascinating."

"I don't think luck had a lot to do with it. Thanks for doing this so quickly. The fact that you're interested makes things a lot easier."

There was that becoming blush again. She gave a little nod. "Then you think this will work?"

"Absolutely. We're using the glass cases at the library, right?"

"Yes."

"Then I can contribute some of the testing gear for more visual interest."

"And if you give me the titles of the journals and books you regularly use, I can pull copies to visually show the resources the library has."

"Can do."

This was turning out a lot better than he had expected. And she'd only frowned at him once. Progress on all fronts.

***

"So-o-o how's your new neighbor?"

Marian grimaced at her sister's question, which was said in a noticeably nosy tone and accompanied by a sly smirk. Iris sat across from Marian at their favorite coffee shop, both drinking coffees. Iris preferred dark, black, and with a bitter smell that pinched Marian's nose even at a distance. This was a routine on Saturday mornings for them both, meeting over coffee and sharing the events of their weeks. Marian sipped hers—mild, decaf, sweet, and heavy on the latte—and considered how much to share with her sister.

Iris was so much like the larger members of her floral namesake, tall and showy, with a mane of auburn hair that Marian would consider selling her grandmother's pearls for... if she thought the sale would do any good. Today Iris wore a turquoise dress with a fitted bodice and ruffled skirt. A brightly colored shawl, a present their mother had brought back from her last honeymoon trip to Mexico—fourth husband, third honeymoon—added light to the cloudy February day.

And Iris had pinned a yellow ranunculus to the shawl. As the owner of a successful flower shop, Iris promoted fresh flowers whenever she got a chance.

Marian sighed, knowing her sister was waiting patiently for an answer. As much as Iris loved flowers, she adored gossip, especially gossip about Marian, and she'd want all the details of the new neighbor. Which Marian was reluctant to share for some reason.

Just thinking about Burt—Gill, she reminded herself—Dr. Gillespie made her stomach quiver.

"He's nice."

"No, sorry. Won't cut it." Iris pointed her index finger directly at Marian. "That's what you say when you don't want to say anything. Or when the topic is interesting, and you're trying not to be enthusiastic. Which is it this time?"

Marian gave up. Gill's behavior was unsettling, and who better to share with than her sister? No matter that Iris viewed the world from a different perspective, Marian depended on her honesty and open heart.

"He's a lot noisier than the Landers." At her sister's snort, Marian laughed. "Yes, I know, anyone would make more noise than the Landers. It's more like he's always... there. Somehow."

"Like how?"

"There's pounding like he's building something. And people coming and going."

"What kind of people?"

Marian's eyebrows shot up. "How would I know? I'm not perched at the window watching. I have other things to do. Then there's the music. All the time."

"What's he listen to?"

"Country. Hard Rock. Jazz. Lots of rock. All hours."

"A man of many tastes. Like you, I might point out. Has he complained when you play the piano?"

"No, but I don't play at all hours."

"What's his name?"

"Gill Gillespie."

"Gillespie. We went to high school with a Gillespie. Burton? Looked great in tennis whites?"

"That's the one. Goes by 'Gill' now."

"Well, the name's certainly an improvement. Wasn't his middle name Edsel? Guess he wouldn't want to use that."

"No, probably not."

Iris sat up, and Marian's heart skipped. "Wait. Burton Gillespie. Your high school crush, right?"

Marian covered her face with her hands, desperate to hide the blush burning her cheeks. "Right."

"You were so in love, it was pitiful. And cute." Iris reached over and pulled Marian's hands away from her face. "We've all had one of those, Sweetie. At least you never had a 'Garth Vader.'" Iris leaned back and took a sip of coffee.

"No." Marian's blush died quickly at the name. Iris's college romance had exploded once Iris had learned the guy planned to propose to her—the devoted, always available woman—but keep playing the field. It still angered Marian that her sister had been the dupe in such a hurtful cliché.

Finally, Iris sighed. "Burton changed his name, huh? If I recall, the rest of him didn't need any improvement at all. What do you think? Does he need any improvement? Other than the noisy part?"

Marian considered a moment and shook her head. Iris's eyes drifted to the window, then back to land on Marian. "What are the odds?"

Here it comes.

"I'll bite. Odds of what?"

"You." Iris grinned. "Living next door to one of the hottest guys in high school. And still hot twelve years later? What a waste."

"A waste? I don't think I—"

"If I lived next to him, you can be sure I'd have no complaints. He could play any music he wanted, just so I could go over and ask him to turn it down. You're missing a huge opportunity here."

"I am not you."

"Yes, many years of sisterhood have established that."

"You will be happy to hear," Marian put in, "I have not missed any opportunity. Remember that collaboration project that I signed up for? With Dr. Abrams?"

Iris nodded. "To pump up your application."

"Seems when Dr. Abrams had his heart attack, Gill took over."

"Ooh. Then Gill was a little gift from God, I'd say."

"I'd be more inclined to believe the gift idea if the walls of the townhouse weren't so thin."

Iris chuckled and leaned back in her chair, her fingers slowly rotating the coffee cup.

"Come to church with me tomorrow. You can pray for rescue from the noise pollution. Or..." Iris drew out the word. "Pray that you'll learn to appreciate hard rock."

Marian laughed and shook her head. She heard a sincere request behind the teasing. Even though Iris asked for Marian's company at services regularly, Iris knew how Marian felt about the mega-church her sister and mother attended.

To spend time with her family, Marian had gone last week, braving the thousand worshipers up on their feet cheering, praying, singing with the encouragement of the band and 100-member choir—as if she wasn't getting enough musical entertainment during the week. Add in the enthusiastic minister so sure of everything, booming his sermon across the vast expanse, the mammoth TV screens. Iris and their mom loved it.

For Marian? The experience had never touched her spiritually. It only made her feel more different. More alone.

Once every six weeks or so was enough for her.

She shook her head and gave her sister an apologetic smile. "Not this weekend. I'm going to sleep in tomorrow and ride my bike down to the beach. Take a nice long walk."

Iris shivered. "Br-r-r. Too cold."

"The word is 'brisk,' sister mine. Brisk."

"Nope. Cold. And I'm sticking to it." Iris laid her hand over Marian's on the table. "I'll send up a few prayers that your neighbor makes a little less noise and you two can get along."

Her sister's expression radiated love, and Marian laid her hand over Iris's. With Iris doing the praying, there was a good chance God might answer.

But in this situation, would it be an answer Marian could live with?

CHAPTER FOUR

Put Your Ducks in a Row

"I do want to bring up one thing before we get started today."

Standing just inside her workroom, Marian sent up a swift prayer, determined to state her case but hoping for a little Divine support as she faced this outgoing, good-looking, infuriating... partner, work colleague, neighbor. For this conversation, she needed a neutral term.

"Okay." He regarded her as if there was nothing wrong. The smile he had greeted her with downstairs lingered. In his world, there probably wasn't.

"I'm- It's very distracting." He tilted his head, and Marian took a breath. What was distracting at this precise moment was the color of his eyes. Deep blue-gray watching her, holding a puzzled look. "The music," she tried. Regrouped. "Not the music, exactly."

Why is this so hard?

She crossed her arms. She wasn't in high school anymore. She was an adult. All right. So what if he was standing there looking all approachable? And very patient. She hadn't practiced her speech enough, she decided, that was it. If his mere walking in the door jumbled her thoughts like this, she should have practiced more. Too late now.

She straightened her spine. "I mean, I like the music. Mostly. But the walls are paper thin." She hesitated, uncertain what to say next.

His expression cleared. "Oh, right. Too loud? Too much?" She bit her lip, and his smile dissolved into a neutral professional demeanor. He nodded. "I get it. Sorry. I didn't know. Except for the occasional piano playing, I don't hear anything at all from your side, so I assumed the insulation was good. I'll take it down a couple of notches."

The loss of the smile and his business-like reply made her regret she had said anything, but really. How did one think with the constant sound? Well, she'd said her piece.

Marian sighed inwardly, dissatisfied with the whole situation. Saying her piece wasn't going to make working together any easier.

They divided up the text for proofing, and Marian started creating template sheets on the computer that would become the final mounting pages for the stamps.

Two hours later, Marian heard the creak and scrape of the chair behind her.

"Let's take a break." At Gill's voice, Marian swiveled around to face him. "We've got most of the text in place," he continued. "I've proofed all of your stamp descriptions, and we've got the stamp positions decided. Do you think we have enough to start printing the final pages?"

"I've still got this last section of text from you to proof. And we need to work on the title page and the final outline."

He grimaced. "My eyes are burning. And I need some fresh air. It's fixin' to be a beautiful afternoon."

Marian grinned at his words. He may have studied up North for his doctorate, but he hadn't lost some of the down-home phrasing. And it didn't sound as if he was peeved over her music request. A blessing in itself. She wanted to co-exist, not be at odds with him.

"Have you explored the pond?" she asked. "There's a nice path that leads through the trees behind our building. We could walk around the path."

"Excellent." Gill stood and stretched.

Marian felt her pulse kick in. He had dressed casually for the early afternoon session, and she had to admit, a pair of cargo pants and a navy tee on his body made a pleasant sight.

In a few minutes, they rounded the building, walked through the grass, and picked up the gravel path that wound through a copse of pines and came out to the edge of a sizable pond, with the path continuing about a half-mile around the edge. Sunlight reflected off the water. Trees shaded the edges marked by tall grasses, a scattering of wildflowers, and clumps of evergreen bushes.

Following the path, they walked in silence for several yards, and Marian realized that after they'd set out to work on their own parts of the project, the workroom had been quiet. Almost as if she had been working alone.

Almost. Although the occasional creak of the chair or shuffle of paper betrayed his presence, a subtle energy seemed to reach across the space between them. A mix of steady mental concentration and warmth. She wondered if her mention of the music had led him to work so quietly. To walk so quietly now. It didn't fit what she expected of him.

Beside her, Gill shifted. "I've been meaning to ask. Your name. Marian. Kind of old-fashioned. Not a name you hear very often."

"My father was a big fan of *The Music Man*. The original with Shirley Jones, not the later Disney version. Mother got to name my older sister, Iris, and Dad named me. And my dad had a thing for blondes."

"And your mother's coloring?

"Blonde."

They exchanged a smile. "Unfortunately, I didn't match the hair-color expectation. Both Iris and I take after Dad. But I did end up as a librarian. Just like the character."

"How long have you been at UNCW?"

"About five years."

"Do you like it?"

"I do. I like the job and the school. I like being in Wilmington, close to family, close to the beach."

A loud quacking broke into the conversation. Marian swung to the sound and pointed. "Oh look. There's Momma with her brood. It seems awfully early."

"It's three weeks to spring, and maybe Papa was taking advantage of the cold nights we've had this month.

As they got closer, the quacking from the mother became more urgent. Marian caught sight of a little one caught in the tall grasses and jogged toward it. "Oh no, one of the ducklings got stuck. Just a minute, sweetie. I'm coming."

In a flash she slipped off her ballerina flats and waded into the low water, feeling the cold seep up her pant legs to her calves. She leaned down to douse her hands in pond water, ignoring the cold. Bending down, she pulled the grasses apart, taking care not to touch the little ball of fuzz beating its tiny wings furiously to get to Momma. Aided by rocking and flapping, the duckling finally maneuvered itself in the proper direction and flopped into clear water, righted itself, and swam away, its little cheeps answered by its Momma, her deeper quacks now sounding calmer.

Marian stepped back out of the water, feeling triumphant, even with muddy bare feet and her light trouser pant legs dripping and soaked up to the knees. After brushing her wet hands down the sides of her pants, she looked up and froze. Gill was staring at her as if she had grown a third eye.

"What?" She straightened.

"That was a great rescue. You do this often?"

She gave a bit of a laugh, unsure whether he was teasing or serious. "Not often. But the little guy was stranded." She lifted her hands palm upwards. "I just couldn't leave him there."

Gill smiled and shook his head. "Of course, you couldn't. And you know it was a boy how?"

She shrugged. "He had gotten lost. Probably didn't ask for directions. What would you think?"

His burst of laughter warmed her through. Gill bent in a courtly gesture. "I bow to your superior deduction skills. We'd better get you home. You're dripping, and the air isn't all that warm out here."

She shivered as clouds moved across the sun, shutting down its bright rays along with the warmth. "Home it is."

As they picked up the pace to retrace their steps, Marian glanced sideways at him. She certainly liked the way he had watched her after she had climbed out of the water, approval mingled with surprise.

His cell phone gave a warble, and he checked the text. "Right." He texted something short and pocketed the phone. "Reminder I have a tennis date after this."

"You still play?"

"Whenever I can. Met up with a college buddy here. Brent Carver. He's in the History department. Do you know him?"

"No. I haven't met him." Except for library colleagues and some of the science faculty, she really hadn't met many people on campus. *I've been here five years. Why not?*

"He plays, and I have to say he gives me a good workout." Gill paused. "Why don't you come? To watch."

Although clouds still blocked the sun, Marian felt the air heat. This guy who ruffled her sleep and daylight hours with unwanted music and dreams was inviting her out on a— Not a date. Definitely not a date. To watch tennis.

"At UNCW?" Marian was relieved her voice sounded so normal.

"Yeah. We would have gone to Hoggard High, but their courts are usually full this time in the afternoon. At UNCW, the Seahawks are still doing indoor drills."

She picked at the cold, wet pants. "I'm all wet."

They had reached the duplex, and Gill walked her to her side of the wrap-around porch. "Get dry and come to the courts when you're ready. We'll play at least an hour, then head out for pizza. Maybe ice cream."

"Pizza and ice cream." She shivered at the thought of something cold. "Is that even a thing?"

"It is with us. There will be other people from the faculty there. Some playing, some not." Then he stopped and studied her, a question on his face. "Unless you don't like tennis."

"I do, actually." When he had been playing in high school, she'd learned all about the game.

"It's usually not a large crowd." His tone held a touch of eagerness in it. "Maybe six of us. Tennis geeks, I'd guess you'd say."

Tennis geeks. Sure, that would be a lot of fun. Arguments rose easily into Marian's mind. *I'm cold and tired. I want to take a shower and pull on some comfortable sweats and read.*

Gill stood in front of her, just waiting. The energy she had sensed upstairs in her office pulsed gently between them. She should just say no.

You're missing a huge opportunity here. Iris's voice came into her head.

He did ask you to go. Another voice, an unfamiliar one, popped in. *To join in.* It had been a long time since she'd accepted an impromptu invitation.

Marian took a breath. "All right."

"Great." His smile broke through as if the clouds had finally passed. "Terrific." He nodded his approval. "Just walk over when you get dried off. If you decide to join us for pizza, I'm taking my car, so I can drive you."

It took her a moment to process that he was offering to drive. "Oh, all right." With a wave, he headed for his own door.

Instantly, Marian felt warmer, not so wet.

By the time she'd taken her shower and walked over to the university courts, the sun had started on its setting arc, but there was still plenty of light to pick out Gill in the center court of three. As she walked behind the tall link fence and passed the near court, she noted two women playing. Small clumps of people stood outside the fences and along the open sides to watch both games.

She found a spot behind Gill's end of the court and in a low voice, asked the woman standing beside her, "Who's winning?"

"Brent is." The woman matched her tone. "Three games to two. Brent needs this point to win the set. They're at 40-15."

Brent served into the net. After watching the ball settle against the net, he pulled a ball from his pocket, tossed it straight up, and directed it down the center line. Gill eyed the ball and positioned himself perfectly for the return shot. They volleyed, and Marian watched both men set up shots and return with precision, their steps fast and powerful.

In high school, Gill had made the State finals, so Marian knew he was good, but to watch his more mature body move with such grace, power, and control took her breath away. *"What a piece of work is man..."* The quotation from Shakespeare seemed more than warranted.

Brent leaned in for a ball that landed just inside his reach, caught the ball with the edge of his racket, and tipped it up, over the edge of the net. The ball dropped just on the other side of the mesh and died.

"Set," Brent called. The spectators hooted and applauded with appreciation. Marian joined in. Even losing, it was clear Gill was a man still maintaining the form and skill that had taken years to hone. She was glad he was still playing.

Gill jogged to the net to shake Brent's hand and swung his arm around the man for a quick hug. "Great game. You were smokin.'"

"Had to save my reputation after last week's disaster."

Both men were grinning as they separated, and Gill walked back to the fence to take a long swig from his water bottle and ruffle his damp hair with a towel. When he looked up, his eyes widened with pleasure. "Hey, you made it."

"I did." She quickly folded her fingers into her palms to quell the tingling sliding up her hands.

"What did you think?"

"I think you have a mean backhand."

He tipped his head. "Thanks. Joining us for pizza?"

"Sure." She watched him towel off. "Are you going to shower first?"

"No, not today. Won't need to with the air so cool. By the time we get to Pizzetta's, I'll be dry."

As Gill had said with his invitation, he drove, commenting on the standings of the current New Hanover High tennis team. They were at the restaurant in under five minutes and soon the eight people—four tennis players and four of the cheering squad— were seated around a table. Gill took the chair beside her, and she could feel the heat radiating from his body as well as an earthy male scent. Distinct, but not unpleasant. She was glad he hadn't taken the shower.

Marian Marie! Get a grip!

She sat back in her chair to take hold of her thoughts and to listen to the conversation. Over pizza, there were stories of previous tennis matches, but because the faculty members were from different departments, they also shared their progress on their research. She asked questions when Andrea, who had stood beside her at the courts, mentioned her interest in the international political situation during the Vietnam War era, and Marian enjoyed the exchange.

When Gill brought up the project he'd gotten "roped into" by Chairman Salazar, all at the table commiserated with similar experiences. Then Gill launched into a description of how he got the best of the deal because of Marian and the duck stamps. Suddenly Marian was the focus of attention, and she glanced around judging how quickly she could escape.

Brent asked, "What duck stamps? Like one of those ink stamps Gisele uses in scrapbooking?" He glanced at the woman at the far end of the table.

"No," Gill answered. "Postage stamps. Tell them about it, Marian."

She saw the interested expressions around her and found encouragement there. "Well, Gill said he was doing research about how ducks are the carriers of unique Influenza A virus strains." She clasped her hands together under the table. Thank heavens no one could see them tremble there. "I found the species Gill studies pictured on stamps from all over the world, so it seemed a good way to illustrate the exhibit poster." The people still seemed interested, so she continued. "The administration is eager to connect with the community, so I've informed the local stamp collecting group. Gill and I have also discussed the possibility of entering the exhibit at the Southeastern Stamp Expo in Atlanta next January."

"These stamps are amazing," Gill broke in. "Like miniature works of art. Marian's going to make my research look very good."

"I can almost see the tenure vote now, Gill," someone commented, and general laughter arose. And as the pizza slices disappeared, Dennis from English sitting beside her, and Gregory who taught German sitting across, asked Marian about the stamps. In between bites, she answered.

And enjoyed herself.

On the ride back to the duplex in comfortable silence, Marian considered that the hour or two in company had been the most fun she had had in a long time.

"Thank you for the invitation," she said as they climbed the porch stairs. "I had a good time."

"I'm glad. They're a good bunch, and I'm lucky Brent and I have known each other for a while. He got me connected to this group."

"Well, thanks again." She was acutely aware of him, standing under her porch light in sweats and a hoodie, his brown hair mussed and his slate blue eyes shining like pools in sunlight. This evening, he had smoothed her way to be part of the group.

She let a smile grow on her lips. "Good night, Gill."

"Good night, Marian."

What a skill, she thought, to put people at ease like that. *To put me at ease.* She closed the door on the evening air, turned the lock, and leaned back on the solid surface.

What a guy!

CHAPTER FIVE

I Don't See an Ugly Duckling

Once the samples are collected and the ducks are safely back in the water, we move to the laboratory and use the latest analytical techniques to determine if a new combination of viral material is present. For the last several years, we've seen no new strains, and could give the All Clear for those flu seasons. If we do find something novel in the future, we'll follow the procedures laid out by the CDC and other health agencies to formulate the attack against the new threat.

Gill lifted his hands from the keyboard and stretched out his fingers. Then he placed his hands together, palm to palm, and separated his fingers like a fan, rolled out his wrists until only his fingertips were touching, then rolled his fingers and palms back together.

"What are you doing?" Marian's voice came as something of a jolt from behind him.

He had been working on the exhibit text, trying to keep the words within the blocks that Marian had created on the screen, and she had been mounting the stamps they had agreed upon. They had worked in complete silence for almost an hour.

"Hand yoga."

"Really? Ooh. Show me." With a twirl and a shove of her feet, she pushed the rolling chair backwards across the floor toward him, swinging neatly around at the last moment to stop just beside him.

Gill blinked and let out a breath. "Lucky for me, you've got some wicked chair moves."

"No luck involved." Her eyes sparkled. "Why do you think the floor here doesn't have carpeting? Got to get in my practice for the next Rolling Chair Championship."

She was joking. With him. Gill wasn't about to let the moment pass by.

"And there is such a thing? A Rolling Chair Championship?"

"The ARCC. For the American trials of course. Surely, you've heard of it. Proponents from the Rolling Chair Council have applied for status as an Olympic sport. I've been doing my research."

"Of course, you have." He smirked.

She held out her hands. "Hand yoga, please."

"Right. OK, put your hands together like you're going to pray, fingers to the sky. Now spread your fingers apart. No, just your fingers. Now roll your hands away from each other, slowly, palms first, all the way up your fingers until only the tips are touching. Did you feel the stretch on the way?"

"I did."

"So, repeat what you just did backwards." While he demonstrated, Marian followed his movements with the intensity she seemed to bring to all she did. No wonder she was a good researcher. "And back to praying hands."

"That feels sensational. Hand yoga. I'd love to know the physiology behind the whole concept."

"Of course, you would."

She blushed. "You're teasing me."

"I am. But only because I'm in awe. You're always learning, exploring."

"It can be distracting. But I love to find out about the world. About life."

"I'd guess that's what drew you to librarianship."

"Actually, my biology professor suggested it, smart man that he was. He could tell I wasn't suited for lab research. I'm not the dive-in-until-you-know-everything-about-one-tiny-aspect-of-the-universe kind of person."

"Like I am."

"Exactly. He thought I could take my love of science and my curiosity and direct both in a profession that encourages interest over a wide range of topics."

"And here you are. Mounting stamps about ducks and flu virus."

"And here I am."

A sensation of contentment washed over Gill. Here was a woman with whom he could share many moments of this... contentment. His skin started to tingle, and his awareness sharpened. Kind of like the time in Canada when he had come upon millions of Monarch butterflies preparing to migrate across Lake Erie. The bright orange and black of butterfly wings had covered every inch of the trees around him. Experiencing something so unexpected, so wonderful could make the world shift into sharp focus.

He grasped his knees and squeezed. The silence had stretched too long.

Marian was rolling slowly back to her side of the room. "Thanks for the hand yoga."

"My pleasure."

He watched as she spun and leaned over her work table, her materials and stamps laid out around her, and sank back into her work.

Gill drew in a breath and let it out slowly. He hadn't known any woman who was so self-contained, who didn't need much attention.

But she had rolled over to find out what he was doing. Her curiosity was something he could relate to. And then she joked with him. Whatever had been bothering her about him when they first met must not be bothering her anymore.

That was a relief. He liked her company a lot when she loosened up. Did her joking today mean she might like his company? Maybe?

He might need to indulge in a bit of research of his own.

***

On Sunday, Gill stood in a group of four parishioners in the lovely Episcopal Church he'd found two years ago when he'd first moved back to Wilmington. He had not wanted to attend where his parents attended and had gone "church-shopping." After a few visits, he had chosen this smaller parish on the Cape Fear River. He listened as the group shared their plans to join several churches in a candlelight walk for social justice planned for the following Saturday. Gill agreed to add his efforts with social media and plenty of promotion to the other Episcopal congregations in the city. For him, his spiritual home also allowed him to put his faith into action.

He backed away and almost ran into a woman passing him. As the scent of a light, classic fragrance wafted by, he caught the woman by the shoulders to steady her and himself.

"Oh, sorry."

Instantly Gill recognized the low voice with a husky note. His gaze met deep brown eyes, and his grip tightened.

"Marian."

"Gill!" Those eyes widened, and she backed out of his grasp with a jerk. "What are you doing here?"

"I attend here. This is my church." He crossed his arms, feeling defensive at her abrupt movement away from him. He had thought they were beyond that, but perhaps the hard contact was enough to put her off. He smiled with what he hoped was friendliness. "What brings you to our church?"

She looked everywhere but at him, her hands clasping and re-clasping. Then she brought her gaze to his. "Visiting. It's my first time. And Haley, there," she gestured back toward the welcome table by the double-wide glass doors, "was kind enough to give me a gift and information." She held up a pink gift bag.

Gill's body flared with a special glow he had experienced before. *No doubt about it. God moment.* God was definitely watching out for him. She had come here, of all places. When he couldn't seem to get her off his mind.

"Let me add my welcome. And if you haven't gotten tired of me yet this week, we could sit together."

As Marian's shoulders lost their tenseness, Gill's own body relaxed. Her warm smile reminded him how pretty she was when she wasn't frowning.

"I'm not tired of you yet, and I'd love to have company."

He gestured as an invitation to walk with him, and they moved through a wide doorway and into the sanctuary.

What would she think of this, he wondered?

She would see the cross first, and knowing its effect, Gill slowed when he heard her quick intake of breath. Plain and majestic, the eighteen-foot-tall ancient symbol of faith stood outside the church but was framed by the wall of windows just behind the altar. The room's modern lines and movable seating added to the sense of openness, as did the stained-glass windows lining both side walls. The space could comfortably seat 200, and the cushioned chairs were positioned in a semi-circle around the altar set on the low stage.

Gill led her to his favorite spot, near the front, on the curve of the semi-circle. Here she'd be able to watch people around the room. He hoped the vantage point would make her more comfortable, as it did him, and provide an instant sense of connection.

***

"This is lovely." Marian kept her voice low as everyone else did, but the rumble of conversation was like a warm blanket.

She settled into the chair, accepted a prayer book from Gill, and took a minute to look at the printed order of service. After her last visit to her family's church, Marian had felt the urge to explore other, smaller churches in Wilmington. Her reading had led her to try St. Mary's-On-the-River.

The organ at the front played the opening bars of a hymn. The tune sounded familiar, and she rose with everyone else.

Following the congregation's lead, she watched the priest and worship leaders process down the center aisle.

From that moment on, her senses were filled with low-key ritual. Call-and-response prayers. Several Bible readings. The music was provided by a small but joyous choir who led the congregation in song, and the service involved a lot of sitting and standing. Through the entire service, the constant was Gill. Guiding her gently, showing her where they were in the prayer book, his arm brushing against hers as he swayed while singing.

In this place was a sense of order that was so different from the mega-church. For her, this felt more intimate, more connected.

Marian could see that Gill fit in here. She had thought to see him at one of the larger churches amid the bustling noise and energy, but here, she sensed a deep stillness in him that worshiped with a balance of energy, reflection, and scripture.

"Do you think you might come back?" he asked as they later headed for the doorway.

"I think I just might."

He gave her a grin, and her body lit up from inside. She had harbored no idea he had this level of—what was the word? Devotion? Seriousness? She had always known him as a social creature at ease with people. She knew he could work with great focus as he did on the exhibit. Here she got a glimpse of the stillness underneath which had her shifting her perspective of him. He might be more like her than she had thought.

"Coffee?" he asked in the lobby.

The new view of Gill, the service, and the strain of the new experience caught up with her. "No, thanks, I think I'll head out. Thank you for sitting with me."

"You're welcome."

"See you later?"

"You don't have a choice." They shared a grin.

He hesitated as if he wanted to ask something. Invite her to brunch, she thought, with a wave of surprise at her own conjecture.

Get a grip, Marian! He's your neighbor. Your work colleague.

The moment passed, and they exchanged a casual wave. In minutes, she was in her car, driving home practically on autopilot while pictures flashed across her mental landscape.

At church, he seemed to know lots of people by name, and they knew him. Not just for a quick hello and off to some other activity but checking in on a deeper level. She could see in her mind's eye, his first attempts at mounting some of the stamps, his fingers less than agile. A surprise because she'd seen him handle chop sticks with ease. Which brought up the take-out they had eaten during one typing session on the project. And him barging in one afternoon, his hair spotted with purple paint, asking for help to sop up what he'd spilled in the bath. Walking by the pond when they took a break, feeding the ducks. His stunned expression after the duckling rescue. His smile. His laugh. His attention. His intelligence. His spiritual center.

She pulled into her driveway, turned the key to OFF, and sat with her hands in her lap.

Was she falling for him? No, couldn't be. Not again.

She sat a little longer.

Wow.

CHAPTER SIX

If It Looks Like a Duck and Quacks Like a Duck, It Still Might Not Be a Duck

Gill stood in front of the glass case that had been assigned to them for "Ducks with the Flu," the working title he and Marian had adopted during an evening of too much work and too little sleep. Sounded like the title of a bad country western song, but they hoped to keep it if an administrator above their pay grade didn't insist on something stuffier and more formal.

Gill crossed his arms. "How high is it?"

Marian let the retractable tape measure snap back into its heavy yellow case. "Thirty-two inches."

"Too short."

"By two inches."

"Who told you thirty-five in the first place?" Gill heard the snap of accusation in his voice but couldn't control it. They needed thirty-four inches for the frame that held the exhibit pages.

"The specs from the manufacturer." Marian's tone had gone rigid. He recognized it and the frustration behind it. "But that seems to have been the measurement to the outside edges. Inside, we lose two inches because of the way the glass panels bump in. I would guess that most of the time it isn't a real issue."

Gill let out a long breath, attempting to blow out some of his nerves with it. "Well, it's a good thing we got the keys and checked now. At least we have another week to decide how to fix it."

They both eyed the case. Gill could almost see the wheels of Marian's mind whirring. When you needed a solution, you just had to give her some time, and the woman delivered. Every time.

He glanced over. She wore a dress sporting a row of buttons and looking like one of his better shirts. The dress fell to just above her knees, fit loosely, even at the belted waist, and disguised what Gill imagined might be a nice figure underneath. The pale orchid color washed her out. Not that he was given to fantasizing, but he did wonder why a woman with so much going for her—those terrific eyes, shiny brown hair, and clear skin—would dress in so unflattering a fashion. No matter her fashion sense, the woman had a certain beauty and remarkable intelligence. Both beckoned him.

"So, got any ideas?" he asked.

"I'm thinking we can split the pages into two panels instead of the one. Stretch the display across the whole case."

"The two panels back-to-back, maybe? Since the case has glass on both sides?"

She nodded. "Yes. That would work, with the other visual aids to the side of the panels."

"You did say you wanted the stamps under glass. Do you have frames for this?"

"We could use clear plexiglass. Have it cut to size? Less weight, which would be a plus, and the protection we need."

That beauty and intelligence urged him to voice a question he hadn't even realized he wanted to ask.

"Hey, I wanted to ask you." He waited until she relocked the glass display cabinet and faced him, her chocolate eyes still lit with the pleasure from solving the problem. He realized he enjoyed seeing that pleasure in her face.

"I've got this wedding to go to on Saturday. My cousin. Sort of a duty thing. It would be a lot more fun if you were there." As he said the words, it flashed through his mind that it really would be more fun. He'd love to hear Marian's take on that side of his family tree. "Will you go with me?"

She stared at him for a moment then flushed and dropped her gaze. Those mental wheels were running with the pace of a hamster.

God. I've lost my mind. Gill slid his hands into his pockets. *Did I just ask Marian Fletcher to be my plus one?*

Both prayer and plea it might be, but God didn't answer.

Would it be fair to subject her to my family who are difficult at the best of times?

Her eyes, wide with a sort of wonder behind them, locked on his. Time paused. He took a breath.

"Yes. I'd like that." Her soft reply sparked his heart.

Time resumed.

He didn't need a cosmic answer.

I did ask her. Because I like her.

Because I don't have to make up conversation if I don't want to. Because she likes ducks and science. We work well together, and she has no idea how beautiful she is. And she doesn't ask me, nag me to take her out, go to parties, change. I can be me with her. She'll sop up paint and keeps a home so tidy it makes my skin itch.

And I want to see if this liking thing has legs on it. Has somewhere to go.

I need to see if I have somewhere to go. With her.

"Great."

***

I have lost my mind.

Marian swung in front of the full-length mirror to study her reflection at different angles. The dress was a shade of blue that her sister had urged on her last year, saying that it brightened her face. She had to admit it did. But it was a V-neck. Lower cut than she was used to and flowed close to her body so that she could feel the soft lightweight fabric brush her legs as she swayed.

In their last phone conversation, she had pointed out to Iris that she had more angles than curves, and the beige summer sheath hanging in her closet fit well. Iris had nixed that idea as outdated, which Marian had corrected to "classic." Iris argued for the blue. Marian gave in when Iris agreed that the beige sandals she already owned would be fine.

Heaven only knew why she had accepted the invitation to his cousin's wedding.

Except that Gill had seemed to want her to go. Duty, he had said. Family obligation, perhaps. She knew what those were like. He had added later they could make it a celebration for the "almost-complete" exhibit, as if he needed more persuasion himself.

She had always assumed that Burton Gillespie would jump at any chance to party. But Gill Gillespie, PhD, faculty member, was different. He did like to celebrate, she thought, even when a task wasn't complete. Had even baked cookies when they had finally decided on the page layouts.

When she had asked about the cousin, he had said he didn't even like the guy. No wonder he suggested another reason to celebrate. Not very promising.

It would be a lot more fun if you were there.

That... well, that was very promising.

Marian moved to the dresser and eyed the jewelry in the small cedar box lying open on top. She fingered a chain of silver she could wear as a necklace and let it puddle on the dresser.

Back in front of the mirror, she pulled her hair on top of her head. Dropped it. Pulled it up again. The dress needed something. Better hair? Frankly, she didn't know what to do with her hair. Her mother described it as "straight as a poker" as if that were a fatal flaw of character. And why was she fussing with it anyway? She had brushed it, made sure it was clean, and used the conditioner Iris suggested. What more did she need?

She thought of the silver hair clip her father had bought her for her birthday the year he had died. She had never worn it. It was much too fancy for work and didn't really go with her little black dress that she wore to every formal function she attended. Not that there were that many of those.

Well... maybe...

She pulled the clip from the box. The artist had crafted the intricate silver filigree into the shape of a butterfly, its wings spotted with tiny bits of colored glass and poised for flight.

You and I, Marian. We're like peas in a pod. We'll just let your mother and sister be the social butterflies of the family.

Her eyes burned.

I'm proud of you, Marian. Never doubt that.

Tears ran slowly down her cheeks as the butterfly blurred in her vision. She found a tissue and wiped her face, grateful she hadn't put on any make-up. With trembling fingers, she gently outlined the edges of the butterfly's wings.

Marian could now recognize that her father's death had ripped her confidence in who she was out from under her. Her dad had been the quieter one, the one who read, who loved science. The one person in the family like her. After his death, she didn't care about clothing because he hadn't. She didn't want to go to parties because he hadn't. In the end, her mother had left her to her own devices to choose what she would wear, what she would do. Losing her father had been a blow from which she had recovered by putting on a blanket of quiet control.

She turned back to the full-length framed mirror hanging on the wall.

She brushed one side of her long hair back and up, catching the brown tresses in the clip. She tilted her head. Considered the whole ensemble. That looked good, she decided. Better than good.

It hit her as hard as that softball Iris had once hurled at her in childhood anger.

This. This is why she had accepted Gill's invitation.

For the first time in a long time, a handsome man she respected had asked her out. Not just as a favor, she sensed, though he had taken that tack, but because he was testing her. Testing them. Testing to see if the smoothness of working together might translate to a social situation, specifically a wedding, that would surely be part of any future they might have together.

And *that's* what the woman in the mirror wanted. To shake off "Marian the Librarian" and find out if there was another

Marian underneath. A woman who tried pretty clothes and a new church, dated, met with friends. Had a social life.

Feeling more confident, Marian applied light make-up just as the lady at the cosmetic counter had showed her. As she stood before the mirror again in the flowing dress, beige high-heeled sandals, and her hair graced by a butterfly, Marian smiled.

She was attending a wedding with Gill.

Gill. Is that why I'm doing this?

She touched the butterfly hair clasp. No. Gill was a catalyst, but she had set herself on this path.

She could do this. She could experiment. Maybe she'd find that she liked a more social life. Maybe not. But at least she was willing to give herself a chance. She was still afraid, nervous.

But then Marian opened the door to Gill's knock and watched his eyes widen and rove quite boldly over her.

"You look lovely." His voice poured over her like warm caramel.

Oh yes. She was going to enjoy exploring a new side of herself. Right by his side.

Some sixty minutes later, after a brief church ceremony and ride to the reception venue, Marian decided that by Gill's side was a good place to stay. As she had suspected, she knew hardly any people in the crowd of over one hundred, and as Gill made the rounds and introduced her, she brought out her standard phrases then fell silent as these people, his people, kept up running conversations about acquaintances and topics she didn't know anything about.

Inwardly, she applauded Iris's taste. In her new dress, Marian felt comfortable and understood a little more about the "female armor" her sister often touted. The conversations never let up while they filled their plates at the buffet and sat around a table for eight that ended up with twelve people around it. When the band finally fired up, the table cleared out, and the deafening, vibrating noise began.

Gill nodded to the dance floor with its bodies and pulsing music and lifted an eyebrow. Marian bit her lip and shook her head.

Gill leaned in. "Not your style?"

She thought she had gotten over her uneasiness with this part of herself. "I don't dance." A ridiculously private confession to make shouting over the noise. "At least, not very well."

He shrugged and smiled. "I don't think many of them dance particularly well either." He gestured to the floor. "To this music, you only have to get up and move to the beat. And I know you have rhythm. You play piano. So, if you want to give it a try, you just let me know."

"I don't think so." She gave him what she hoped was a reassuring smile. "But please, I don't mind if you do."

He watched her, looking for something she couldn't begin to fathom. He must have been satisfied with what he saw, since he nodded then moved his chair in close to hers. "While we're watching, let me tell you some stories about these people."

Sitting beside her, his arm around the back of her chair, their bodies touching and the warmth of his breath caressing her cheek, he pointed out relatives and friends, shared how he knew them, and launched into stories that always ended in her laughing. With his information in hand, Marian felt more at ease to converse as the music segued through pop hits and rock and as the faces around the table changed. Gill did dance with women whom she now recognized as relatives or friends. While Gill was dancing with his sister, Marian left to get two more glasses of cold punch and wove her way back through the crowd.

A knot of bodies and a familiar female voice stopped her.

"I thought you were bringing Natalie."

"That's right. *You* thought I was bringing Natalie."

Gill. Cold liquid sloshed over Marian's hands. Gill and the woman stood side by side facing the crowd. From Marian's position behind them, she couldn't see the woman's face. But she wore a lovely dress of pale violet with a sheen to it and had medium blond hair that streamed to her shoulders in perfect waves. It came to her. Gill's sister had visited their table for a while. Connie, Carrie, *Claire.*

"I was surprised," Claire continued. "I can't keep up. Who is this one?" Her belittling tone confirmed the identity of the speaker.

"Marian Fletcher. She's my neighbor at the duplex. That's how we met. I'm working with her on a project at work."

"Oh. Someone from UNCW, I guess?" A beat of silence was followed by, "The duck thing?"

"The duck thing."

"Oh, but Gill, she's so quiet. Doesn't she ever talk?"

Marian cringed.

"Claire, do you think I would ever date someone who didn't talk? She talks plenty to me."

"Doesn't she dance? You love to dance."

Marian frowned. He did. He enjoyed himself on the dance floor. Marian could tell. Where did that leave her? Standing in the crowd holding cold drinks in her now sticky hands. Not on the dance floor. She waited for Gill's reply, shifting a little to edge closer.

"There's more to life than dancing. When did you become the dating police? Oh wait, I know this one. When you were six. I was four, and you hit Theresa Moffat for playing with me. Lighten up, Claire."

"Theresa's family lived in the next neighborhood."

"You're a snob, Claire, do you know that?" The words had no heat in them, as if this were an old topic between them. "I love you like a sister—oh yeah, you are my sister. But you're a snob."

Claire punched her brother's arm. Marian saw a gap in the people-knot she could wedge through and escaped, her thoughts tossed together like confetti.

When Gill arrived back at their table, Marian hoped he saw a poised, unperturbed woman nursing her drink and watching the dancing. The music changed, slowed. Gill gave her a slight smile and held out his hand. "Shall we give this a whirl?"

A slow dance. This she could do.

Even better, she found she could do it with him. He was as good a slow-dancer as fast, no surprise there, and easy to follow. She relaxed, found the rhythm with him, and together they moved smoothly in small spirals around the floor.

"And you said you can't dance," he whispered into her ear.

"You're easy to follow."

"Years of training. Too bad my mother, the social taskmaster, isn't here or you could thank her."

"Perhaps I will."

He pulled her into a turn and settled her in his arms.

Secure in the dance, Marian's mind took off. His sister didn't like her. He loved to dance. He moved easily through crowds. He came from a well-to-do family. She had known that in high school but had never cared. No need to care about those things in fantasyland. Maybe she should care now? He had a lot of friends. Natalie, for one. How close a friend? Close enough for a "plus one" assumption.

Go away!

She tightened her grip on Gill, and he pulled her in just a little closer.

Right now, his arms held her in a warm embrace. They were dancing. On air. This was one of those "feeling times" as her sister called them. And right now, she liked the way she was feeling.

She needed her Scarlett O'Hara impression. She'd deal with her doubts tomorrow. After all, tomorrow was another day.

CHAPTER SEVEN

Oh Lordy, There Be Ducks Here!

As Marian sat in Gill's four-wheel drive in the Croatan National Forest, darkness and silence surrounded her like a heavy carpet. At this hour before dawn, all life slept. As any sane person would be doing. She shifted. Any doubts from earlier in the week had been replaced by doubts concerning her sanity.

"Remind me again how you talked me into this?"

Sitting behind the wheel, his elbow resting on the open window, Gill chuckled. "In the name of science. Adding our efforts to prepare for the next flu epidemic. A chance to handle the live ducks you collect on stamps."

"Oh, yes. Now I remember."

"Sounds like someone needs more coffee."

She waved off the thermos he offered. "I've had way too much already."

Her nerves hummed like live wires. Knowing she would be buzzing with enough excited energy all day to power a small town, she should have held to only one cup, but Gill had brought a thermos with the liquid caffeine light and sweet. After the first luxurious taste, during the two-hour drive to the Croatan National Forest, she had nearly emptied the thermos. It was her own fault if she was jangling.

"How much longer?" she asked. Her heel bounced in a frantic rhythm.

"Under an hour. The ducks will arrive as the sun is rising." He placed his hand on her knee. "No more coffee. You are officially cut off."

She heard the laugh under his words. *Talking.* She might burn off some of the inner buzz with talking. "No more coffee. Agreed. I'm nervous, too. You've done this before. I don't know what to expect. So, I know we're testing blue-winged teals. And that they migrate long distances."

"Carrying the flu virus," he put in.

"Carrying the flu virus. And tell me again how they'll catch the ducks? You said, 'rocket net capture'?"

"There are rockets connected to the leading end of a large net. When the ducks have all bunched up at the site, the team shoots the net over the ducks, keeping them in the water. Then the team wades out into the pond, untangles the ducks from the net, and puts them in those square yellow keeping crates you saw in the back of the trucks."

"And we're waiting for them to bring the crates holding the ducks to us so we can help with the sampling."

"Yep. There's enough dry land here for the testing set-up. You got it."

"The ducks must be terrified when they're netted."

"I'm sure it's unsettling, but they're not hurt. And the crew will work quickly to remove them."

Thinking of the little guys floundering with a net over their heads, Marian shivered. In the darkness, she whispered the question hanging in her mind. "Do you ever feel like that? Like you're caught in a net?"

The silence pulsed. *Oh Lord, I've done it now. Never drink caffeine and ask.* Marian wondered if she should take back the question. Gill's quiet voice reached her out of the dark.

"I have. When I was living at home. The Gillespies are a prominent family." He paused, and Marian sensed him gathering his thoughts. "When you grow up in a prominent family, there are expectations, an image to uphold. Decisions already made for you. I've heard some of my cousins talk about feeling suffocated. As if they couldn't breathe. For me, I could breathe just fine. But I could see the world through the gilded net, and I wanted to make my own decisions."

"Is that when you started using 'Gill'?"

"It was. We were studying fish during marine biology, and my lab partner decided I should be 'Gill,' and it stuck. Burton's my dad, so I decided, what the heck? New life path, new name. UNC Chapel Hill instead of Ivy League. Basic science instead of politics or law. Ended up at the University of Maryland for graduate work."

"Then you came back. Back into the net?"

She watched his profile in the now-gray light. She could see his lips move into a smirk. "Let's say... beside the net. I make forays in every once in a while, but on my own terms."

"And your cousin's wedding? 'Net' duty?"

He laughed and shifted in the seat to face her. "I like that. Net Duty." The laughter faded as his eyes caught hers. "I wouldn't have gone if you had said no."

He reached over and took her hand, bringing warmth to the conversation and reassurance.

With his hand still over hers, he asked, "And you? Are you... caught in some way?"

Caught. The word stopped her. Caught by him? She couldn't deny the thread that pulled between them. She watched him a moment. No, the serious tone in his voice held no flirting. No hint of teasing. "I-I have been. For a long time. I've been kind of stuck. Since my father died."

"How old were you?"

"Twelve."

"Hard age."

She nodded. Looking back on that time, she could acknowledge the truth. "Life just stopped somehow. The net landed over me. I could see the world from my ordinary net—" She gave him a small smile which he returned. "But I didn't want to leave. There's a fair amount of safety in staying the same."

The squeeze of his fingers against hers gave her the courage to look straight at him.

"But it feels like I've been pulling the net off little by little. With you."

His palm rose to cup her cheek, and she raised her hand to lay it over his and lean into his touch. His hand slipped to the back of her neck, and he pulled her toward him. At the urging of his motion, thought swept away. Eyes locked to his, Marian placed her hand on his shoulder and followed his lead. She closed her eyes and moved closer, impatient for the inevitable.

A gunshot pierced the air.

Gill froze. Marian's eyes flew open to see him scanning the now visible landscape outside the truck. When he faced her again, his lips held a rueful smile, and he stroked his fingers down her cheek. "Afraid that's our cue. We'll pick up where we left off later, shall we?"

Feeling more of the net slip off, Marian grinned, tugged his head so his lips met hers in a quick kiss. Into his stunned look, she said low and soft, "Absolutely."

Both grinning, they pushed open the SUV doors, and with his hand in hers, Gill led her along a dirt path through the thick pines to the gathering area beside a broad stretch of marsh.

They approached a group of eight men and women, some in camouflage—hunters, Gill explained—others in jeans, t-shirts, and light jackets against the early morning chill. As they were introducing themselves, deep rumbles brought the group's attention to the two trucks trundling up at a steady pace, their open cargo holds packed with two dozen yellow crates, the high quack of the captured ducks breaking through the deeper sounds. As the crates were unloaded, a woman disengaged herself from the action and headed to their volunteer group. She walked with a confidence Marian wished she had. But Gill had explained that Jess had been doing this kind of field work for over fifteen years, so this was familiar territory.

As the library was for her, Marian thought.

"Hi everyone. I'm Jess Stander from the North Carolina Wildlife Commission, and I'm the field veterinarian for this collection. I recognize some of you from last spring. Good to see you again, and thanks to everyone for coming out. Here's one of our ducks for the day." She held up a duck that fit neatly between her hands. "You can see how I'm holding it. Head's facing outward so it can see. I've got my hands firm enough around the wings, so the duck has some movement, but the wings are pinned. And I've got my pinkies wrapped around the legs to keep them out of the way."

Marian watched closely. So far, it seemed easy enough.

"So, for today's collection, here's the process. Kelly and Brad over there by the crates will pull out a duck, band it, and record it. Kelly will hand the duck to you and tell you the number of the band. Remember the number, look at the band if you have to. Bring the duck to Donald over there. Don't even think of joking." A ripple of laughter rose, and Donald gave the group a bow. "Donald will ask you the band number and draw blood from the duck. Then you bring the duck to me, and repeat the band number, and I'll do the throat and cloacal swabs. That's a butt swab for those who don't know."

Marian flinched. *Ouch. Poor ducks!*

"Then I give you the 'Okay,' and you can let the duck go. Any questions? All right. Let's get to it."

The "holders" lined up for what one of the hunters called the "Duck Assembly Line," and Marian peered around the people in front of her to get another look at the hold. Directly in front of her, Gill took his duck in a solid grip, the duck quieting in his large hands. Then, Marian stood in front of Kelly, and the young graduate student handed the next duck over. From the prominent white band down its face, Marian silently classed, *male.* She slid her hands around the duck.

It fluttered. Marian's hands slipped, and the duck ended sort of sideways. Pressing the duck against her body, Marian repositioned her hands.

Kelly said, "Pinky fingers under the legs."

With another awkward turn of her hands, she got the legs secured. Kelly gave her the thumbs up, and Marian followed the line to Donald's station. As she stood waiting her turn, the duck squirmed a bit then settled.

The little guy's heart was beating triple time, and it swiveled its head, no doubt looking for escape. The feathers under her hands felt smooth, and his duck body gave off a warmth and vitality that awed her. She was holding this living, breathing creature, and coming to understand on a primal level how intertwined she and the duck were in the web of life. The enormity of the connection, of the pulse of life under her fingers, of the community of scientists working conscientiously to help prepare the world for an unseen, unpredictable invasion brought tears to Marian's eyes.

This was God. Here in her hands. In the hands of these volunteers. In this forest with its lakes and pine trees and marshes. In the scientists' efforts. In the man standing in front of her waiting his turn.

She blinked hard. She felt part of the divine plan, working for something much larger than she could ever envision. For the first time in her life, she felt certain she'd be able to push away the rest of the net and discover who Marian Fletcher was and who she was meant to be.

As Gill took up his duck, he straightened to face her. "How's it going?" He frowned. "Hey, you okay?"

Even though her vision blurred, she beamed at him. "Just ducky."

He laughed and headed off to the final collection station.

Five hours later, all the ducks had been tested, and, in what Marian learned was an informal tradition, the whole team lined up at the water's edge with the last of the ducks, and on the count of three, released the happy waterfowl into the air to join their companions and complete the spring migration.

They finished by washing up with bottled water, mild soap, and sanitizing gel.

Still full of the joyful, spiritual experience, Marian walked hand in hand with Gill back to his SUV. He opened her door, but before climbing in, she stopped to study his face.

"I had a wonderful time today." He leaned back against the open door, his arms loosely crossed. As a smile grew on his lips, her throat dried up, but she swallowed and hurried on. "It opened me up somehow to see the world in a way I never have before. So full of life and good work and good people willing to participate in making it better. Thank you so much for inviting me. And driving. And..."

You're becoming so important to me. Maybe too important. But I'm taking a chance.

Marian reached out to lay her hand on his arm. "Just... thanks."

She hadn't said any of the things she had been thinking. Yet from the glow that now lit his eyes to warm, dark pewter blue, she knew he had understood. In a smooth motion, he left the door to place his hands on her shoulders with the same care he had given the ducks earlier.

"You're welcome," he whispered.

His lips met hers without a hint of hesitation. Unlike her earlier quick, teasing touch, Gill's kiss settled on her mouth, weaving together desire and commitment. He wrapped his arms around her, and Marian leaned in, gathering him in at the same time, welcoming the embrace, reveling in the feel of sharing breath, sharing life. The wired buzz of the pre-dawn hours was back, only now the product of this strong man's body, hot and damp from the day's exertion, his arms holding her.

And through his kiss, Marian drank in the unspoken declaration that he was willing to take a chance on her, too.

CHAPTER EIGHT

How About I Just Duck Out Now?

On Wednesday night, Marian unlocked the door of her townhome, feeling light and airy all over. Gill had lost his tennis match, but the company at Pizzetta's had been as loud and excited as ever, and the breeze was just right to bring with it the salt tang from the ocean. She felt Gill's hand on her arm.

"Can I come in a minute? I've got something to ask you."

He seemed hesitant in both his voice and manner, and Marian's pulse sped up at his unease and what the question might be. He followed her in and shut the door but stayed close to it as if he planned a quick escape.

Marian took a steadying breath and gave him a tentative smile. "What is it?"

"I-um got a call from my mother earlier today to remind me about this fundraiser she and Dad are hosting on Friday night. I've backed out of most of the charity circle, but this happens to be an event to support the North Carolina aquariums, and it's being held at the Fort Fisher Aquarium."

"So, Duty Net." Always a loaded topic with Gill. Perhaps some levity would help. "And you're all about the fishes. Or fish viruses?"

"Fish don't carry Influenza A, so no. But I'm a fan of the aquarium and as a fundraising venue, it's pretty spectacular."

She nodded. "Duty Net with benefits."

He smiled at that. Marian relaxed a little. Until he said, "Even more benefits if you come with me. Would you be willing to go?"

She held her body still to hide the nerves that jittered inside. Another foray into the Duty Net with Gill. Their conversation on Duck Day, as they'd started calling it, nudged her. Duty Wedding two weeks ago. Now Duty Fundraiser.

Not my definition of "forays every once in a while."

"This Friday, you said."

"Yeah. Short notice, I know. Too short?"

Depended on the...

"What's the dress code?"

"Black tie. Women wear long gowns."

Marian paused, momentarily impressed that he specified the women's attire. Training from his mother and sister, no doubt. Mentally, she scanned her closet. She had... nothing. Absolutely nothing. "Did you say your parents were hosting?"

"Their Foundation is, so they'll be there."

And I'd meet the parents. Her heart skipped a beat. *At a black-tie affair. In two days. For which I have nothing to wear.* She clasped her hands together. Maybe she had been silent too long, or Gill had sensed her anxiety, but he had started talking again, persuading.

"It won't be much different from the wedding, really. Different people. A lot more glitter. Less fun. Business friendly, I guess. I'll be expected to mingle and encourage people to open their wallets, but you won't have much to do."

"Arm candy, then."

He had the grace to look sheepish. "Does sound that way."

Diving into his world. At the Aquarium. Which I also love. As arm candy. She took a breath to loosen the tightness in her chest. *I wanted new experiences. No time like the present.*

"Alright. Okay. I'll go. I guess."

"You will?" The relief in those words and the pleasure on Gill's face relieved some of her own tension. Gill pulled her in for a long, tight hug. "Thanks. A lot. I appreciate it."

Even as she snuggled into his embrace, drawing in his warmth, a chill flowed through her.

I'm going to meet his parents. Good heavens, what will I wear?

Iris! Help!

***

Marian watched her sister shuffle deftly through a rack of glittering, shining evening gowns.

"I owe you." Marian held her breath as Iris stopped at a pale green dress, heavily flounced and ruffled. She was not wearing ruffles. Absolutely not. When Iris slid the dress aside, Marian's breathing restarted.

"Are you kidding? You call, totally frantic, asking help from *moi* to choose a gown for the city's most fabulous charity event of the season. I'm on it like white on rice."

Marian pursed her lips. "I was not frantic."

"Honey, you were frantic." She shuffled more dresses across the rack. "Not to worry. Sissy Iris will take care of everything. Aha!"

With that exclamation, Iris pulled out a gown of Chinese blue. "Hold out your arms." Iris placed the dress on Marian's outstretched forearms. Another dress of eggplant purple followed, and one more of deep rose. Not a ruffle in sight, Marian noted with relief, although a flounce seemed to dominate the bottom of the purple item.

In the oversized dressing room, the purple and the Chinese blue received instant thumbs-down from Iris, an opinion Marian shared. Marian considered the deep rose dress on the hanger. A soft waffle shirring covered the corset-like bodice held up by two wide fabric strips that crisscrossed in the back. The long skirt fell in a soft A-line to an embroidered, scalloped hem. The moment the soft material slid over her and she guided her arms through the crisscross, Marian's excitement rose.

As Iris adjusted the dress on her shoulders and the skirt dropped into place, Marian heard her sister sigh. Marian turned and faced the wall mirror. The cut of the bodice was high enough to assuage her more conservative streak, and the shirring allowed the material to fit her curves with a flattering softness. Her cheeks had taken on a faint echo of the dress's deeper rose. Her eyes shone like polished walnut.

"Let's go look in the big mirror," Iris urged.

In front of the three angled panels, Marian could easily see her back which, except for the crisscross, was bare almost to the waist. A lot more skin than she usually showed, but perfectly discreet under the wide, rose-colored X. The long line of the skirt continued the soft fall of color to her toes, and when she swayed, the scallops floated lightly around her ankles.

"Nice." Iris commented from behind her. Their eyes met in the mirror. "That new haircut is terrific with that dress style.

And I've got a pair of dangly earrings you can borrow. That's all you'll need."

Iris had insisted that she have her hair cut and styled. Marian had balked at taking it too short, but the stylist had cropped the bangs and given her a modern layered shag that had enough length to satisfy both her and Iris. Now, as she swayed, her hair moved subtly with her, the shorter layers flowing gently around, settling back into place when she stopped.

Marian swung to face her sister. "Thanks for bullying me into the salon."

"That's what older sisters are for." As Marian swayed to display the front of the dress to Iris, her sister added with a grin, "The perfect dancing dress."

Dancing with Gill, Marian thought. At a charity event sponsored by the Burton and Dottie Gillespie Charitable Trust. Gill's parents. The uncomfortable chill that had haunted her ever since Gill had asked her to go, slithered through her now.

She watched the dress as she swayed. The sleeping princess in the tower had faced a paddling of ducks, visited a new church, and was beginning to appreciate flattering clothing. Now she would face a bigger challenge.

The full experience of a major society event.

Even with Gill there... Just ducky.

***

On Friday evening, Marian opened the door to Gill wearing a three-piece suit in a deep blue that darkened his eyes to navy and highlighted all the wonderful lines of his body. Then she noticed the tie displaying swimming ducks. The whole effect both weakened her knees and delighted her. *Perfect.*

"My parents sent a car."

Marian checked out the street where he gestured. *His parents sent a car.* No, she amended, they sent a limousine shining brilliant white under the late day sun. Maybe the sleeping princess would rather have a nap right now.

When she turned back to Gill, she noticed his eyes were raking over every inch of her and glowing like blue steel. With him by her side, she could do this. She gathered up her gold and silver wrist bag and a lacy shawl made of white and rose thread so airy she could barely feel the weight as Gill laid it on her shoulders.

Settled into the oversized back seat of the limo, sitting with space between them, Marian shifted on the smooth white leather, felt the thick carpet tickle her toes in her open sandals, and brushed her fingers against the polished wood inlays in the door. The driver pulled the limo away from the curb and headed out of the city, south toward Carolina and Kure Beaches.

"Would you like something to drink? The minibar has wine, soft drinks, and water."

"No, thank you." She was terrified that she might spill something on her dress. Or on the white leather. Or on the thick white carpet. She just wanted to sit here and absorb the sensations and the splendor, trying to orient herself to this alternate reality. Gill in his home territory.

His hand slid over hers. "Nervous?"

She dipped her head then nodded as she met his gaze. "I am. A bit. I've never been to anything like this before."

"You have nothing to worry about. You look stunning, so you've already mastered the arm candy, and I'll be doing the heavy lifting."

Glowing at his compliment, she had to laugh at his teasing words. "And what's the heavy lifting tonight?"

He shrugged. "A little ego-stroking, a little friendly encouragement, making a connection between the person giving and the charity."

"You need to know people to do those things."

He nodded. "Works better if you know the people personally. Otherwise, you need a cause you believe in, which I do, then learn to read people and recognize the best way to persuade them. My mother is a master of that."

"And your father?"

"No slouch. But for these things, he takes Mother's lead. She thrives on this."

"I'll be glad to meet them." And she would be. It would give her another view of this man who was fast becoming a necessary part of her life. A man who made her insides quiver for so many reasons.

Only a half-hour later, with Marian's hand under Gill's arm, they climbed the broad stairs to the front entrance of the aquarium. Gill presented their invitation, and they followed other attendees through the Cape Fear Conservatory, an exhibit dedicated to the land-based flora and fauna of the Cape Fear River basin.

As they sauntered by the box turtles, alligators, and snakes, Marian sighed. "I haven't been here in ages. I came on field trips in middle school and once in college, but for some reason never got back."

"How about we come back another time and really explore?"

Marian squeezed Gill's arm. "I'd like that."

As they neared the end of the walk, Marian heard the chatter of voices up ahead. A few steps through a wide entranceway, and they entered a different world.

For the Aquarium, that meant the marine life off the North Carolina shores, but to Marian, the new world included a crowd of people as sparkling as the viewing glass of the large exhibit tanks and the glasses of wine many in the crowd held. Marian had a good idea of how Cinderella felt.

Gill placed his hand over hers where it lay on his arm, and she realized she had tightened her grip. Her Prince Charming was beside her, but as soon as Marian entered the crowd, the sense that she didn't belong engulfed her. She fit in, thanks to the new hair and dress—*thank you, Iris*—but mingling with this many people in one place gave her butterflies.

Gill threaded his way to an older couple standing near a short flight of stairs leading to the "Shadows in the Sand" exhibit.

As they approached, the tall women with rich auburn hair pulled into an elegant French twist held out her hands to Gill in welcome.

"Burton, darling. How wonderful to see you tonight!"

Gill walked into her embrace. "Mother, it's good to see you, too." He stepped back to shake the man's hand. "Dad."

"Son. Glad you made it."

The man Marian assumed was his father gave Gill a warm smile in a face that seemed made for happy expressions. No less elegant than his wife, Gill's father wore wealth like a familiar overcoat on his sturdy frame.

Gill reached out his hand to Marian. Introductions coming. She took the offered hand eagerly, needing his touch to anchor her while her mind bounced through several impressions.

Mother's acting the hostess. Some nerves, excitement underneath? So elegant. Dad's got a great smile. I might like him.

Gill squeezed her hand and cleared his throat. His hand felt damp in hers. *Nerves, too?* Marian glanced at him. He straightened.

"May I introduce Marian Fletcher? Marian and I went to high school together. She's my neighbor in the duplex and a work colleague. Marian, Mr. and Mrs. Gillespie."

He didn't include "friend" in that introduction as he normally does. Just "neighbor" and "colleague." Why?

Mrs. Gillespie offered her hand. Marian automatically took it. The older woman's expression matched the coolness of her grip. The coolness seemed to brush over Marian's skin.

"A colleague? You're a professor at UNCW?"

Marian pulled her hand back as she felt Mrs. Gillespie's grip release. "I'm a sciences cataloger at the Randall Library, Mrs. Gillespie. Gill and I are collaborating on an exhibit to highlight the interactions of the university's departments."

At Gill's given name, his mother's eyes narrowed. But all she said was, "I see."

Marian turned deliberately from the woman's eagle stare to her husband. "Mr. Gillespie, a pleasure to meet you."

"My pleasure as well, Marian." She saw where Gill had gotten his eyes. His father had them in the same silvered blue. The lines around them crinkled in true pleasure. "Sciences. Then you must be involved with his flu research."

Marian could feel a frown aimed in her direction from his wife, but she gave Mr. Gillespie a smile. "Your son has been orienting me to his work. We've even been out in the field together."

The man's eyebrows furrowed, and he glanced at Gill. "The ducks?"

She felt Gill's arm come around her shoulder. "The ducks. Marian came with me on the sample collection last week."

"And it must be so convenient that she lives right next door." Mrs. Gillespie's undertone held vibrations Marian didn't understand. The woman peered over Marian's shoulder. "Here come the Nagles. Make sure that you circle the room, Burton. You know why we're here."

Gill nodded. "For the aquarium. Of course."

His mother beamed. "And don't forget to talk with Natalie. She's been looking for you."

Marian's ears perked up. *Natalie.* Gill's sister had mentioned a Natalie. As his expected plus one. Old friend? Girlfriend?

Gill squeezed Marian's shoulder, but said only, "We've got our marching orders, Marian. Best get to it."

"Good to meet you both," Marian managed as Gill steered her away.

"Whew," Gill whispered. "Got away easy."

"You looked nervous. Were you?"

His eyes widened. "I was, but I didn't think anyone would notice."

"I was holding your hand."

He gave her a rueful smile. "Right."

"Why so nervous?"

He rubbed the back of his neck. "Don't know. I guess... It's been a long time since I've brought—well... someone to one of these things."

He didn't bring Natalie? Or hadn't in a long time? Old girlfriend then. Marian gave herself a mental shake and thought of Gill's nerves. "I like your father." *Not so sure about the mom.*

"I do, too." He scanned the room and gave a decisive nod. "I have a plan. Let's get something to drink, make the rounds, and move on."

No mention of Natalie in the plan, Marian thought. Claire's comments at the wedding rang in Marian's mind. The crowd sparkled and buzzed around her. I'm not ready to open that can of worms yet, she decided.

"Lead on."

CHAPTER NINE

Ducks Can Fly Only When They Are Free of the Net

To Marian's surprise, Gill led her to a table set with silver tiers of finger desserts. There they enjoyed mini eclairs, which he claimed would give him the energy for the next stage of the evening. Fortified now and with wine in hand, he scanned the room.

Marian's curiosity got the best of her. She ventured, "Looking for Natalie?"

"What?" He glanced at her. Continued his scan. "No. I'll catch her later."

So, no rush, Marian thought. Maybe avoidance?

As they made their way slowly around the room, Marian soon recognized his pattern. Gill would choose a group in which he recognized someone. Then he deftly moved to the known person and made the first greeting. Introductions followed. Gill always mentioned his connection to the elder Gillespies, made sure everyone knew Marian was with him—although the "friend" word was still not used, Marian noted — and guided the conversation to the aquarium. And to donating.

It bothered her for some reason. No word of acknowledgement, of attachment. His kiss at the end of Duck Day had held all the marks of commitment, an exclusive relationship.

But let's be honest, you're not experienced enough to know for sure. Let it go, Marian Marie!

Circulating was interrupted by a loudspeaker announcement to gather in the auditorium on the lower level. To the well-heeled audience the elder Gillespies gave short speeches, thanking everyone for coming. A five-minute film presented the Aquarium's plans for the next year, and the Aquarium director rose at the end to thank everyone in advance for their generosity.

As Marian and Gill left the auditorium, Gill suggested more eclairs, but no more wine.

"How're you holding up?" he asked when they reached the dessert table.

"I'm good." Her low, glittery sandals were comfortable, and though she felt dazed, she realized not much was expected of her. She wondered if that was all right with Gill. He didn't seem bothered in the least by her lack of social support.

"We hit everyone I know upstairs. Let's see who's down here."

Gill offered his arm, and they moved on. On this lower floor, they wound their way through exhibits of sea horses, moon jellies, dolphins, and whales, pausing when Gill recognized someone or when an acquaintance stopped him.

Introductions, handshakes, encouraging a donation, laughing. Often a check changing hands. Then smoothly making excuses and moving on. He was like a politician in high gear, giving the impression that even for the short interaction, each person was important. This was the social guy Marian remembered from high school. Comfortable in crowds, easy with friends and strangers alike, on a mission.

Marian wished she were anywhere else but here.

As another conversation drifted around her, Marian studied Gill and compared the man standing beside her to her neighbor, the intense, quiet guy who worked without a word for hours at a time. He might say that forays into the Duty Net were on his terms, but did he realize that when he was on duty, he was all in, completely immersed?

The whole experience had her mind whirling so that it was increasingly hard to bring words to her mouth.

Her speaking, or lack thereof, made no difference. Gill carried them along on a cloud of words and body language that she at once envied, marveled at, and inwardly cringed over.

Once, Gill changed direction abruptly. "Sorry. I saw Natalie." He gave Marian an apologetic smile. "She'll tie me up for at least twenty minutes. I'll catch her later to give her the checks I've collected tonight."

Natalie. Again. Avoidance for sure. Marian knew she had to get to the bottom of the Natalie story, but not here. Marian was on sensory overload as it was, and she didn't need an emotionally draining conversation in the middle of an event. But soon.

A voice hailed them from behind, and as they turned, Gill moved forward to grasp the man's hand.

"Orin! Man, you are a sight for sore eyes. Glad you could make it."

Gill introduced the man and his companion as Betsy and Orin Smith. In comparison to many of the attendees, the Smiths were closer in age to Marian and Gill. They had been part of the country club crowd Gill had hung with many eons ago, as he put it, and Orin usually joined them for the weekly tennis sets.

"I've missed you out there on the courts."

"Thanks," Orin replied. "Sorry. Had a lot to do, but I'll be there next week."

The two began talking tennis, and Betsy pulled Marian aside. "They'll be at that for a while. I want to know more about you. What keeps you busy? Other than attending this event with Gill."

Marian couldn't stop a blush from rising. "I'm a Cataloger at Randall Library. I work with a lot of sciences materials. Right now, Gill and I are mounting a library exhibit about ducks carrying new flu virus strains. We went on the sample collection last weekend." As she added this last, almost by rote, Marian realized a lot of her recent time had been spent with Gill. Was that a good thing?

Betsy was regarding her with a narrowed gaze. "You did, did you? Out at Croatan Forest?" Marian nodded. "Well, that's interesting."

Marian tilted her head and waited a beat before venturing, "Interesting?"

Betsy moved in a little closer and quirked her index finger. Marian stepped in. "The story around the country club circles for years has been that Mrs. Gillespie planned on Gill and Natalie Carson tying the knot. They've been dating forever."

Marian lost all her words, stunned that a friend of Gill's was willingly pouring out information about Natalie *Carson* for her, a near stranger introduced as Gill's plus one for the evening. He and Natalie getting married? Dating forever? And he'd never said a word. As a chill crossed her shoulders, Marian glanced at Gill. He was sharing a laugh with Orin.

What *was* the story between Gill and Natalie?

Marian swallowed. "I-I've never met Natalie."

"No surprise there. She avoids campus like the plague. I can point her out." Betsy's gaze swept the room. Marian suddenly didn't want to know what the woman looked like. She was about to protest when Betsy touched her arm.

"By the Cape Fear Shoals exhibit. Near the end of the room? Tallish, honey blond. Wearing the shimmery blue creation with all the fringe.

Since the Shoals exhibit lay up a short level from where she and Betsy stood, it was easy to see above the mingling crowd. The dress caught Marian's eye first, the rows of blue fringe swaying with every movement of the woman's body. And she moved quite a lot as she talked to her male companion, using both hands and hips for emphasis. Marian took in the whole effect. Merciful heavens, the woman was gorgeous. Model-stunning. Her movements fluid, her body a study in subtle curves. Marian stole a glance at Gill. Oh yes, she could see them together. The glowing blond hair beside his deep brown. No wonder Dottie Gillespie wanted Natalie as a daughter-in-law.

The vision made Marian ill.

Something must have shown in her face because Betsy said quietly, "Gill brought *you* tonight. That probably landed like a rock on Dottie Gillespie. And you can be sure he never took Natalie to the Croatan Forest. She wouldn't be caught dead near a body of water that wasn't a hot tub."

Despite the uncertainty crawling through her, Marian had to laugh. She studied Natalie of the Blue Fringe again. No, she couldn't see the woman holding ducks on a marsh.

Not very charitable, her conscience piped up. *You don't know her. Maybe she loves ducks.*

Sorry. She probably looks terrific in rubber-booted chest waders, too.

Better.

It didn't make Marian feel any better. She was still irked.

"I'm heading for the Ladies Room."

Betsy gave Marian a knowing look. She waved her hand in the direction of the two men. "I'll let him know."

When Marian glanced at her reflection in the bathroom mirror, she marveled that her face wasn't glowing radioactive green. She washed her hands slowly, giving herself time to settle. While she dried them, a memory flowered in her mind.

"Don't make comparisons, Marian." Iris had used her Mother voice with a waggled finger for emphasis. "Just remember, the world is full of 'different pretty.'" Marian had tilted her head at her sister's phrasing. "Every girl can be pretty. Some have model-pretty. Others have cute-pretty. Girl-next-door pretty. Handsome-pretty. If you discover what you have and work with it, you'll find your own version of pretty, and people will see it, too."

Different pretty.

Marian stood and peered at her reflection. She wasn't Natalie. Not light-haired, model-pretty. Marian decided she had natural-pretty with a quiet intelligence.

She was Marian Fletcher. And she was just fine the way she was.

The bathroom exit let her out near the gift shop doors, and from there she could see across the length of the room. No Betsy or Orin. No Gill.

Without thought, she glanced back up the ramp to the Cape Fear Shoals exhibit. The crowd had thinned, leaving a clear sight line. Natalie still stood there.

Talking with Gill.

For a moment, Marian considered striding up the ramp and getting an introduction. Facing the woman who had been—

Marian halted her steps and stared.

Like watching a romance movie, Marian saw the ease with which they interacted, how Natalie leaned toward him, touched his arm with a familiarity that suggested a long-standing relationship. Gill didn't step away, didn't remove Natalie's hand to break the contact, but continued to listen with the attention he also gave to Marian.

Sadness tugged at her, and a needle stung her heart. That attention was something she loved about him... but not exclusively hers, it seemed. Natalie was *still* a part of Gill's life at some basic level.

There were smiles between the couple, the Woman of the Blue Fringe and the handsome man in coordinating blue, but no laughter. Gill shook his head in a chiding way, said something close to her ear, then gave Natalie a hug and kissed her cheek. As Gill walked down the ramp toward the gift shop, Marian watched as Natalie noted his progress, her expression a mix of calculation and longing. She had seen that same longing in her sister's eyes. During the "Garth Vader" time.

Natalie loves him.

Marian swung to take a few steps into the gift shop, lingering at the wall baskets holding stuffed marine-life toys. She studied the sea turtles, dolphins, and alligators without seeing them.

Even if he considers himself free, Natalie doesn't.

Marian's heart cracked a little. *You're playing a 'Garth Vader', Gill.* Memories of Iris's tears and hurt ran through her. Holding her sister as the pain poured out.

And I can't consider you free either.

Tears burned behind her eyes, and she furiously blinked them back. Was his behavior unintentional or deliberate? Didn't matter.

Then he was beside her.

"There you are. I passed all the checks I had to Natalie, so I'm done for the night. Are you ready to leave?"

She found a smile to hide her unease. "Yes. I think I am."

Settled back in the limousine heading north, amid the silence, elegance, and subdued light supplied by small ceiling lamps, Marian mind raced for a way to bring up the subject. She sensed Gill shifting in his seat. His voice rose softly out of the quiet.

"I think that went well. I'll check with Mother in a couple of days and see how we did." Moving closer, he took her hand. "Thanks for coming with me," he whispered, his eyes shining silver blue. He leaned toward her.

Kiss! Can't!

Before his lips could reach hers, Marian pulled back.

Gill froze. His forehead wrinkled. "Marian?"

She took a deep breath, prayed for the right words. Pitched her tone as normally as she could. "Why didn't you tell me about Natalie?"

He leaned back and after a moment, frowned. "There isn't anything to tell."

"Except that you've been dating for years, and your mother is planning the wedding."

"Who told you—?"

"Does it matter?" Her hands trembled.

"I guess not." He huffed. "Two important points. First, my *mother* is doing the planning. Second, I'm not engaged."

"Perhaps not officially, but if your mother is planning, how does Natalie feel about that?"

"I don't know. We don't talk about it."

"Don't talk about the fact that your mother is planning a wedding? For the two of you? I don't think that's possible."

"There's no reason to. Natalie knows I'm not going to propose to her."

"Then why hasn't she told your mother to stop? Or asked you to talk to your mother?"

He stared. The purr of the tires and engine echoed the tense silence between them.

Unintentional. Clueless. There was some relief in that.

"There is still something between you two."

"Of course, there is," he protested. "We've been friends since grade school."

More complications. More cords between them. She gave a sigh and waded into the discussion's murky water. "Tell me something. Did you enjoy yourself tonight?" When he started to speak, she cut him off. "Honestly."

"Honestly?" He shrugged. "Not particularly."

"But you put on a great show. No one would have guessed that this event was part of your Duty Net. It was like watching a play, a performance. Your social mask in place. Except with Orin and Betsy. With them, I saw you again."

"That's the point, isn't it? There is a mask. It's useful for the occasion. Everyone does it."

"Natalie sees the mask. She sees the role you play when you're in the net. Your mother reinforces that because she sees the role, too." She raised her hand to stop his protest. "Neither of them has gotten the message." Urgency made her shift closer to him. "You told me that the forays into the Net are on your terms. Maybe so, but you act as if you're still playing by their rules."

"All evening, I've been your 'work colleague' when I thought we were friends. More than friends. Or did the kiss mean nothing to you?"

"Of course, it did. Marian—"

She grasped both his hands and met his gaze. "I'm falling for you, Gill. But I can't allow myself to fall all the way when you're still tangled up with a woman waiting for you to propose and a mother sure it will happen. Natalie needs more. I need more."

She pulled her hands away and felt a sharp pang in her heart. If she had met him last year, she might have ignored what she saw, too grateful for a man's attention to risk losing it. But this year, these past weeks, had shown her a different path. She was going to walk away. For the sake of a woman she had never met. For her own sake.

Away from the best thing that had ever happened to her.

"I don't think we should see each other. Socially, I mean. Professionally, we'll have little choice. At least until the exhibit is mounted."

While their eyes locked, the air pulsed between them for long seconds.

Gill lowered his head and moved away from her to settle by the door and peer out into the darkness. The limo purred along, stopping and starting as it maneuvered through traffic lights and route turns along the highway.

"If that's what you want," he finally said, watching her from the distance of a car seat that seemed to have stretched to an ocean away.

"Yes. It is."

He nodded. "I guess it wouldn't make a difference if I said I loved you."

She shook her head slowly, tears welling in her eyes. "You're not free."

He nodded again.

They made the rest of the trip in silence. In silence Gill walked her to her door, waited until she unlocked it and stepped over the threshold.

"Good night, Marian."

"Good-bye, Gill."

His eyes widened and reached for her.

Marian stepped out of his reach and gently closed the door. After locking it, she leaned against the wood and prayed for strength.

CHAPTER TEN

To a Duck, Daylight Means Flying.
Nighttime Means Gathering Strength.

For the next week, Gill did as Marian asked. He stayed away. He taught classes, met with students. He went to church.

He played tennis against Orin and noticed Marian wasn't there. He served another ace, and Orin watched the ball fly by with amazement. Orin accepted the loss graciously and mentioned that Gill certainly seemed to be fired up about something.

With Marian only a wall away, the townhouse felt like a steel box. A quiet steel box. He had gotten used to being with Marian. Just being in the same room with her was a pleasure. So, Gill paced and fumed. He strode to the stereo system, hit "play" on the CD player and cranked up the volume. Heavy metal blasted out of the speakers.

There. You can't get rid of me that easily.

He let it run for five minutes.

Juvenile move, Gillespie.

He shut it off.

It just didn't seem fair. He hadn't done anything to hurt her. He'd been considering that possibility for days and came up empty. Anyway, how could he miss someone who wore unflattering, monochrome clothing and had that small, gentle voice. In his mind arose a vision of her standing at the door of her home last Friday night and wearing a gown the same deep burgundy as a rose in his mother's garden named Black

Magic. Monochrome burgundy had sure worked its magic on him. He'd hardly been able to breathe.

She claimed he hadn't introduced her as a friend at the fundraiser. Absurd! Of course, he had. His mind slid across the introductions he'd exchanged during the evening.

His mother and father. He thought back to the nervousness that seemed to explode over him when it was time to introduce Marian. His mind had scrambled as he grasped for words.

Why the scramble?

He answered himself. *Didn't want to face your mother later. Didn't want to face the scene she'd create berating you for your choice outside society circles.*

Her *society circles*, he argued back. *Not mine.*

Not yours? What about your introductions to the other donors, guests?

Surely, he had said "friend."

He shuffled through the evening in his head. No. Actually, he hadn't.

The thought hit him broadside.

Why not?

He had just wanted to get through the entire affair with minimum hassle. Collect the checks and leave. He'd used words like *Neighbor. Work Colleague. The duck project.* Not friend.

She wasn't wrong.

He did consider her a friend. At the very least. In the limousine, he had even admitted that he loved her.

In that rather backhanded way, he reminded himself and grimaced.

Face it, Gillespie, you were running scared all night. Scared of what?

Gill paced the living room. How caught in the net was he?

What if she's right about Natalie?

The voice that spoke softly in his mind held a shimmer under the words that he always associated with a message touched by the Divine.

Letting the question sink in a bit, he headed for the fridge, pulled out a bottle of Cheerwine, and sat in his recliner. He popped the top and sipped. Good old Cheerwine had helped him through childhood, and as he grew older, he realized he didn't need alcohol when he had wild-cherry flavored, sugary fizzy water. So now, he sipped his 'thinking' drink, and he thought.

He'd admit it. There was something between him and Natalie. Why wouldn't there be? He'd known her since they were kids, and when Gill had decided to take a different path from the one his parents had expected, Natalie had supported his decision. Been there for him. Like he had been there for her when her brother had died in that surfing accident.

That's what friends do, right?

He took another sip. And thought.

***

Marian shoved back her rolling chair, and it shot backwards. Startled, Marian slapped her sneakers to the floor and let the rubber soles slow the chair. Instead of crashing into the table behind her, the chair hit with a tap.

Marian dropped her head into her hands.

I did the right thing, didn't I?

She flung the question at herself, the known universe, and God all at once, hoping an answer would materialize and put an end to her constant second-guessing. It had been over a week now, and she hadn't seen Gill. Hadn't heard from him. No texts or calls. He hadn't pounded on the door demanding to be heard. No waving across the connecting porch. No walks by the pond. Nothing. Except for the blast of music on Wednesday evening that had made her drop the fruitwood bowl she had been dusting.

She missed him terribly.

Marian snatched up the cell phone and pressed the speed-dial for her sister.

"Hello?"

Thank the Lord, Iris answered.

"How long will it take him to come to his senses? I'm trying to be patient. I shouldn't have to suffer because he can't see the truth. This waiting is ridiculous."

"Oh, Marian, honey, you've got it bad. It's only been a week."

"Ten days."

"Ten days. Right. Look, he'll come to his senses or he won't. It's out of your hands now. There's no timetable for this kind of thing."

Marian paced her workroom, keeping her distance from the stamp album pages laid out on her table. "It just isn't fair."

"Life is not always fair, you know that. So, let me ask you something."

Marian wasn't sure she wanted to deal with another question, and she disliked the serious tone of Iris's voice. She headed downstairs. "All right."

"Do you think he loves Natalie?"

Marian stopped at the bottom of the stairs. In her mind's eye, she saw the two of them together and tried to pull away the green jealousy filter. "I'm not sure. But she was giving all the signals that she'd like to be more than friends."

"So, not picking up the hints. Typical guy. Clueless. Just like you said. Next question. Do you believe he loves you?"

Instantly she heard his voice, the regret, the sadness under the words.

I guess it wouldn't make a difference if I said I loved you.

She moved and sank onto the sofa.

"Yes."

"Points for him and takes some time off the waiting clock. Final question. How much do you love him?"

Marian sighed. "More than I love ducks?"

Iris chuckled softly. "Well then, I'd settle in to wait for as long as it takes. Although you might want to set a time limit for yourself."

"A couple of weeks?" Marian ventured, hoping.

"A couple of months."

Marian pouted. "It's just not fair."

"I can hear you pouting. Chin up. You're setting up for the exhibit tomorrow night, right?"

"Yes."

"Then play it cool. You're all professional and cordial. You have a friendly working relationship. If he needs neighborly-type help, you can do that, too. All at a respectable social distance. The ball's in his court. It's up to him to serve. And wear one of those new tops you bought."

The thought of her new sleeveless lacy beige tunic laid over a turquoise T-shirt brightened Marian's outlook.

Wonder what Gill would say?

***

Late on Wednesday night, Gill stood on his back porch watching the stars overhead.

What am I going to do?

It was a prayer like many others he'd offered under the stars God had created, knowing chances were slim of a direct answer. He'd get an answer, of that he was sure, when he let God help him out.

I just don't know what to do.

Marian had walked into the library earlier in the evening wearing a stylish, casual outfit with a T-shirt the color of the ocean off the coast of the Bahamas. She seemed to glow from the inside out, and he thought he'd get lost in the chestnut brown of her eyes. He'd barely been able to manage a hello before she had directed him to carry in the other board, if he would please, while she got the keys from the office. Collected, professional, friendly. *Distant.*

They worked together to place the boards, each holding eight pages of stamps and research descriptions, and discussed how to display the other items he had brought. His hands placed things on the glass shelves among the library resources Marian had set in the case earlier. All the while his arms ached to pull her to him and kiss her breathless.

And she didn't seem to be affected at all. Acted as if the conversation in the limo had never happened. As if there weren't days of silence between them. Like colleagues. He cringed and swung away from the view and into the townhouse, determined to put the evening out of his mind. He headed for the fridge, reached for the door handle, and stopped.

Except...

A memory appeared out of the collage of images from the evening.

He had been placing the last items from the lab and sample collection in the case and had stepped back to view the results. Through the glass and the items, he had seen Marian walking toward him. From the time she'd left to verify details with the exhibit coordinator, he'd been waiting for her, Gill now realized. His pulse had kicked up when he had seen her, and worry had caused him to slide his hand through his hair.

Her eyes had looked puffy, and she had tucked a white cloth hastily into the pocket of her jeans. Because of the situation, he had clamped down on his instinct to ask if anything was wrong. When she had given him a smile and asked how it was going, he followed her lead, and they finished their work, but he had noticed that her smile seemed dim and didn't reach her eyes.

No, she hadn't forgotten the limo conversation any more than he had. In her manner all evening, she had been telling him that she still liked him, perhaps loved him, but she wasn't going to nag him like his mother or Claire often did. She would wait him out.

Natalie needs more.

Staying away from Marian was killing him.
What if she's right?

***

Opening day of the exhibits had arrived. Marian stood at one corner of the "Ducks with the Flu" exhibit, ready to answer questions. Gill was talking with a graduate student from his department. He wore a sport jacket, no tie, exuding the look of a typical, low-key college professor. The exchange was animated, but Gill had his hands in his pockets, the sign he was nervous or excited. His outward social ease was unmistakable.

She bit her lip. Goodness, her life had been peppered with more social engagements in the past month than she usually attended in a year. Is this what life would be like with him? Stretches of quiet work and walks, separated by forays into the social network? She couldn't think about a life with him. If he didn't want to change how he spent his time and attention, Marian would be left with acting as if she didn't care. Not a happy prospect.

Her gaze swept the gathering of her UNCW colleagues from all over campus and watched a few members of the stamp club read the exhibit before moving on. A sense of belonging touched her. She realized that for the first time, she felt like part of the community, not just working behind the scenes.

Balance. She was finding her balance.

Dr. Salazar approached the case and began to read. A tingle rode up Marian's spine. Gill's department chair.

"If you have any questions, please let me know."

He glanced her way and nodded, then went back to his study.

Gill joined her, but now she could feel the tension in his body.

After Salazar had perused both sides of the case, he approached Gill, his hand extended. "Dr. Gillespie, good to see you."

"Dr. Salazar. Glad you've come."

"Fine work you've done here. Very clever to use stamps for the illustrations and to broaden the discussion worldwide. Excellent."

"I'm not the clever one in that regard. You know Marian Fletcher?"

"Indeed." They shook hands. "You're the stamp collector, then?"

"I am. It was a happy coincidence that Dr. Gillespie's influenza research included ducks. And several members of the local philatelic society have already visited, so the exhibit is helping to make a connection with the community."

"Don't forget the Southeastern Stamp Expo in January, Marian," Gill added. "That will spread information about the university's programs—and the department's—even further."

Salazar nodded. "Just what the Dean's Office was hoping. It's a wonderful exhibit. A credit to the department, Gill. And to the library, Marian."

"Thank you."

"Perhaps the two of you will collaborate more in the future. Looks like you make a good team."

Gill gave Marian a warm smile before answering. "You're probably right. Marian and I actually share a wall in a duplex near campus. Between living next door and working on this project, we've become close friends."

Marian's heart skipped a beat. He had listened. She gave him a small smile in thanks. "As long as he doesn't blast heavy metal through the wall, it's all good."

Salazar laughed. "Well, Gill, Marian. Let me congratulate you both for a job well done. This will be a good addition to your tenure packet, Gill." He shook hands again, and after the two men exchanged a knowing look, Salazar moved away.

"What was that all about?" Marian asked.

Gill let out a long breath. "My tenure packet. Remember? Salazar had made a point to remind me of the advantages of my participation in this project. He knew exactly the right carrot to hold out. Adding this exhibit to my publications list along with positive student feedback in my tenure packet will give my chances for tenure a big boost. And this will be a boost to your application for Sciences Librarian, too."

"It will definitely help. And if the exhibit does well in Atlanta in January, I'll feel I've honored my father in a tangible way."

"So we both got something out of the effort."

"We did." Behind her smile, Marian's heart ached.

And possibly lost something, too.

CHAPTER ELEVEN

Ducks of a Feather Paddle Together!

Marian checked her calendar. Two weeks since the exhibit opening. Two weeks of minimal Gill contact. Not that she was keeping track.

Thankfully, new booklists filled her "To Be Reviewed" computer tab at work, and she had plenty to keep her mind off Gill. Except that most days, she passed the "Ducks with the Flu" exhibit and had to block out the memories of working with him. She wondered what he was doing. How his research was going. She had received several new books to catalog on viral research and had seen a news article on a new strain of avian flu in India.

She could call him. Let him know. Professional, like Iris said.

Desperate.

She didn't make the call.

At home, there were no more blasts of music through the walls. He was respecting her sound privacy, but she wished he'd violate it so she'd know he was still there. It was almost as quiet as when the elderly couple had lived there.

And she hated it.

She found herself taking more walks, biking to the beach as the weather warmed. She walked long stretches of Wrightsville Beach, glad it was still early in the tourist season and the cooler weather kept the crowds away. She needed a lot of time to think and pray. The ocean always reminded her of the endless power and love of God. On the shore, she talked to God the Father and Mother of life, as well as to her own father, and renewed her determination to choose the life she wanted to live.

The church community at St. Mary's by the River provided spiritual comfort, but one Sunday, Marian saw Gill at the later service. The next weekend, she switched to the early service. She yearned for his company beside her, yet she feared he might tell her he had decided he didn't want her in his life, in his future.

She went shopping with Iris and accepted an invitation to join her cataloging colleagues for their Thursday evening gathering at a local pub. At the next Wilmington Philatelic Society meeting, She found it almost easy to say a few words about the UNCW exhibit and to encourage people to go and view it.

She was discovering a daily rhythm, more connected, more social, more spiritual. Even without Gill in her world, she felt more self-assured day-by-day as she uncovered Marian Fletcher.

On Friday night, Iris called. "Weather's supposed to be great tomorrow. Pack a thermos. Let's bike to the beach early—say about eight and have coffee there. I'll bring the quilt."

"Sounds great." Marian welcomed anything to get her out of the house and away from the silence.

On Saturday morning she pedaled alongside her sister to a spot where there was a break in the coastal string of hotels and vacation rentals. Fewer people used these in-between sections of beach, especially at this hour in the morning. The light breeze, warmed by the sun and fragrant with sea salt, touched her cheeks like a kiss, and Marian reveled in both the morning

God had granted and the love of a sister who knew just how to support her.

After they locked up their bikes, Marian unlatched her beach bag with the necessary sunscreen, towel, and precious thermos. The late April day allowed for a light blouse over capris, but given the sun's glowing rays, Marian had added a long-sleeved cover-up to the bag.

The sisters climbed up the wooden stairs to the raised boardwalk that took them over the dunes covered in waving sea oats, then descended on the other side and stepped into the loose, grainy sand. To her right, Marian peered out over a stretch of sand, yards wide due to the low tide, empty except for a few joggers running at the water's edge. To her left, like an island in a vast sea of sand, one lone man lay stretched out on a towel, his weight propped up on his elbows, his gaze focused on the unending roll of waves.

To Marian's surprise, Iris gestured in the man's direction. "Let's go say hi."

Marian stopped. "No. Iris, we can't. He looks like he wants to be left alone."

"Oh, he won't mind."

"Iris!"

In frustration, Marian watched her sister tromp through the sand. Just before Iris reached him, the man's head swung to glance over his shoulder, and with a smooth move, he rolled to his knees and rose to stand, facing in her direction. Her heartbeat shot to double time.

Gill.

Her sister stood beside him now, grinning. "Come on!" She waved. "Don't just stand there."

They had planned this.

She didn't know whether to be furious with her sister for the ambush, run as fast as she could in the opposite direction, or face the conversation she had yearned for and dreaded these eight weeks.

The Marian of this past winter would have run. The Marian of today's spring took a deep breath. The salt air caught on her tongue. She heard the endless rumble and splash of the low waves and sent up a fervent, "God be with me as you always are," and commanded her feet to move forward.

She divided her gaze between navigating the changing sinking softness and packed hardness of the sand and studying Gill, standing so still and tall, barefoot in jeans and a UNCW Seahawks T-shirt, topped by a denim jacket. The sun shining behind him threw his lean physique into relief. Every nerve ending inside her awoke.

She reached him.

"Hi," Gill said softly.

"Hi."

Marian was close enough to feel his body heat, to see the pulse beat against his neck, to count all the silver flecks that gave his blue eyes their silver-pewter look, to sense his nerves wound as tightly as hers. His eyes made their own inspection, as a starving man might survey a banquet set out before him. Longing radiated from him like a live thing.

Yet, he didn't touch her.

After long seconds, his gaze never leaving hers, Gill angled toward a quilt now laid on the sand, the quilt Iris had brought, and gestured. "Will you sit with me?"

After a nod, Marian knelt on the quilt. As she settled on one hip and arm with her legs folded under her, she saw Iris lift a small canvas bag out of her own backpack and lay it on the quilt's corner.

With that, Iris gave them a jaunty wave. "You kids have fun." She folded her hand to mimic a phone, held it to her ear, and mouthed, *Call me.*

Marian let out a breathy laugh and ducked her head, shooing her sister away with her hand.

Gill joined her on the quilt to sit cross-legged at her side and reached for a tall thermos stuck in the sand. "I'm going to need an extra shot of caffeine for this."

Silently, Marian agreed. Wholeheartedly. Maybe not the best beverage choice given she was buzzing inside already, but the taste and warmth would ground her. She pulled her own thermos out of her beach bag and poured a cup for herself.

Gill sipped and gazed at the beach and the waves. When he faced her, his eyes were pewter-dark.

"You were right," he began softly. "I've been holding on to a lot of baggage from the past."

Marian let out a breath. Here was hope, handed to her on this bright spring day when she had rocked between despair and uncertainty for so many weeks. She nodded in encouragement.

"Natalie and I have been friends since grade school. Her brother died in a surfing accident when we were in high school, and I made sure I was there for her. We were dating off and on, and Mom started mentioning how perfect it would be if we eventually married. I brushed the idea away. I considered Natalie a friend, and we were still young."

Looking back, Marian remembered that the gossip surrounding Gill had mentioned his many girlfriends, not anyone in particular. And she had never heard any talk of an engagement. Granted, she had never been part of Gill's crowd.

Gill took another sip of coffee. "I had already made plans to change directions and head off to Chapel Hill. Natalie encouraged me, stood by me. When I announced to my parents that I was heading in another, unexpected direction, the discussions and arguments took their toll on our relationships. Claire was in her self-absorbed teen years, so all she wanted was for me to soothe the waters. Make the tension go away. By the time I left for Chapel Hill, I had vowed never to return to Wilmington."

"That must have been a hard decision." There must have been many more arguments than discussions. Marian could hardly imagine the pain and guilt that would accompany ripping yourself away from your childhood in such a dramatic way.

"Bad times for sure. In Chapel Hill, Natalie was my lifeline. We kept in touch through e-mail, Skype, texts, letters. She supported me all the way through college and grad school. I owe her a lot."

As Marian listened, sadness rolled over her like cold fog. He had been lonely, separated from his family but determined, and his friend had made his adjustment to life on his own bearable. Going to college without her own family's support? Unthinkable.

"Natalie and I drifted apart once I went to Maryland. We still communicated, but I didn't see her in person for years."

"How did you end up back here in Wilmington?"

"I grew up."

Marian sensed a great deal of self-blame in that admission and could relate to "growing up." This spring had been a growth time for her.

Gill continued. "My youthful arrogance had burned off, I guess. I missed home, missed my family, the beaches. I realized I was as much to blame for the separation from my family as they were. And when it came time to look past my doctorate, I realized I wanted to teach more than anything. You know how it is with the high-powered research programs. Emphasis on publish-or-perish, less on teaching, and I wanted a better balance. I got an offer to teach at Cape Fear Community College a couple of years ago and moved back. That gave me the first step into a smaller school and an emphasis on teaching. Then Dr. Abrams took ill and... here I am."

"Here you are."

Gill smiled at her then, and Marian understood the freedom that telling his story gave him. In sharing his journey, he was breaking open his heart to her and trusting her to hold it. The trust he placed in her was staggering.

"I'd been away a long time, and I had assumed I was coming home with a clean slate. I hadn't really thought there might be lingering expectations. I had built my own life, thought everything was good. With Natalie, there was nothing more than friendship and deep gratitude. At least on my side."

"You didn't realize Natalie loved you?"

A rueful laugh escaped him. "Clueless, right? We were friends. I said as much when I came back. She never asked or even hinted for more." He shrugged. "Maybe I gave her mixed signals. I don't know. And generally, I ignored my mother's broad hints. For me, everything was fine. Whatever my mother assumed wasn't going to happen. Natalie and I never talked about marriage. We dated casually, hanging out with other friends from the country club set. It was all good."

Those gray-blue eyes locked on hers. "Then I met you."

After only a heartbeat, Gill looked away, as if the sight of her burned him. He peered over the stretch of sand, and Marian followed his gaze to watch a lifeguard jeep cruise slowly down the packed-sand driving lanes close to the dunes.

"Walk with me." Gill offered her a hand up. At his touch, something vital in her soul reconnected to his. Something that she had lost and now found.

"Looking back, I can tell that I was drifting. And that drift had pulled with it some outdated expectations. I wonder how long I would have drifted if you had not pointed it out."

"Perhaps you would have married Natalie."

"No."

His answer came with swift certainty, and Marian's heart fluttered. Still she questioned.

"No?"

Gill stopped and tugged on her hand so that she faced him. "No. Really, just no. I knew I'd never marry Natalie. She's totally immersed in the city's society, such as it is, and I had learned that academic life suits me perfectly. My regret is that I let things slide along, hoping that time would resolve any issues with Natalie and with my family."

"That didn't seem to work very well."

"No, it didn't."

Together they walked for several yards until Gill stopped. He took both of her hands in his. "Thank you."

Without more, Marian understood the breadth of his thanks. She saw sincerity in his eyes and felt it around her hands.

"You're welcome."

She studied him a moment, then asked the question that seemed to define her concerns. "And how is that drifting going for you now?"

"I'm done drifting, that's for sure. Did a lot of thinking and realized I would have to do what my father always advised—manage outdated expectations. Cutting the tethers, as you pointed out."

Marian tightened her grip on his hands and held on, sending her love through her touch. His expression told her he had more to say. She gave his hands a tug, took her place beside him and drew him forward. They moved to the water's edge, walking through the shallows, kicking gently at the rippling water.

"I started with Natalie," Gill finally offered, and Marian listened intently. "I went over to her place, and I told her very clearly that I considered her a friend, but that she and I would not make each other happy." He took a deep breath. "There were a lot of tears."

Which Marian suspected he had not enjoyed. "It took a lot of courage to face those tears."

"You're telling me." The low outburst made her laugh. "I hate to see someone I love—even a friend," he quickly pointed out, "in tears."

She gave him a smile to let him know she understood. "And your mother?"

"I decided to kill two birds, and I—" He broke off. "I had promised myself I wouldn't use that idiom. In honor of the ducks."

She thought her heart would burst right in her chest. This was why she loved him. He was such a softy.

"Anyway, you know what I mean. I went to Sunday dinner at my mom and dad's. Claire is always there. I haven't gone in a long time, so I think both Mother and Claire were waiting for the big engagement announcement. First, I made it clear that they might ask me to attend a function, but I would decide whether to attend based on if I wanted to go, not just because of a perceived family obligation. Then, I told them that Natalie and I had agreed to remain friends. And I said I expected them to be civil to you because I would be seeing you exclusively in the future."

Marian squeezed his hand. "You did?"

He chuckled. "I did. Mother gave me her eagle stare—"

"I know that one." Mrs. Gillespie's expression at the fundraiser would stay with her a long time.

"We'll see it in the future, I'm sure. I rephrased. I stated that I wanted to pursue a serious relationship with you, and they had better get on board."

"Serious, huh?"

"Very serious. I'm a free man, and I intend to use that newfound freedom sharing my life with you."

With a turn, he lay both his hands on her shoulders. His touch and the regret in his eyes caused warmth to radiate through her.

"I'm sorry," Gill murmured. "I'm sorry it took me so long to find my way. To you. I want to continue the journey we started together and see where it takes us. I love you, Marian, my favorite, wonderful, beautiful librarian."

He fumbled in his jacket pocket, produced a thin, rectangular white box, and presented it to her.

In the box on a layer of cotton lay a golden bracelet decorated with six charms—one larger mother duck swimming with her four ducklings and one lost duckling swimming several links behind them.

Marian's legs gave way. She sank to her knees in the sand, for the first time in her life oblivious to the sandy slush and the seawater lapping over her capris.

Gill joined her and pulled the bracelet from the box. "Marian, rescuer of ducklings and duck holder extraordinaire, will you paddle along with me? Explore some new waters?"

Tears welled up and fell unheeded down Marian's cheeks.

"Oh no," Gill protested. "You're crying. Don't do that."

"Good tears," she managed. "I promise."

She held out her arm. With a bit of fumbling, the box disappeared back into the jacket pocket. Gill slipped the circlet around her wrist and clasped it. Each duck's tiny face held two small crystal eyes reflecting the morning sun. The ducks tinkled softly as Marian moved her wrist and admired the craftsmanship.

"Where did you get this? It's wonderful."

"I asked a jeweler I know downtown to make it."

Everything in her softened. "Just for me? Oh, Gill, I do love you."

The tension vanished from his face as he beamed at her. Marian threw her arms around him, and he responded with an embrace both loving and protective.

Gill pulled back far enough to find her lips and sealed his commitment with a kiss as tender and light as the spring ocean breeze. Marian's body melted against his.

After several moments of sweet pleasure, Gill took his mouth a mere breath away and whispered, "Is that a yes?"

Marian chuckled softly, brushed her lips against his cheek, then placed her lips close to his ear.

"Yes," she whispered back. "Definitely. Yes. I'd love to paddle along with you. Only you."

Returning to his lips, Marian sealed her own promise with a slow, thorough kiss.

THE END

If you enjoyed JUST DUCKY, would you consider writing a review in Goodreads or where you purchased this book? Reviews are the best way for readers to discover great new books.

But before you go, enjoy this sneak peek at another contemporary inspirational novel created in the Spirit:

The Master's Plan (excerpt)

Contemporary Inspirational Romance
Copyright 2017 LaVerne St. George

Chapter One

Lightning streaked across the sky over the Missouri Ozarks. Thunder rumbled and dissolved into the swaying evergreens overhead while a gust of wind dashed chilled raindrops against Caralyn Masters' cheeks.

A storm, she thought grimly. *Just what I need.*

Frowning, Cara stopped and shifted the heavy backpack on her shoulders. The temperature had dropped at least twenty degrees in the last hour, and the available light faded steadily as the afternoon sun set behind thickening clouds. On her way up the trail the day before, she had seen a sign for a shelter. Now, on her way back down, she had forgotten exactly how far along it was.

She sighed. *I'm out of practice.*

Two years ago, she would have automatically placed the location of the shelter in her mind just in case the weather turned. But yesterday she had done nothing but drink in the scenery. Her six-hour trek up the mountainside had been warm and dry. Vistas of dark green peaks thrusting toward robin's-egg-blue skies had thrilled her at every bend of the path. An exceptional September day. The perfect way to unwind after a day of endless questions and orientation sessions — worth every minute if the Doncaster Foundation awarded her a grant.

Now she hiked down the trail in cold drizzle, picking her way over troublesome stones, kicking others out of the way.

She threw a shuddering glance at the two-hundred-foot cliff dropping away to her right. One misstep and she'd break her neck on the slippery path before she found a place to sit out the storm.

Another flash of lightning brightened the somber sky and lit a wooden trail sign. The shelter lay just a quarter-mile to the left. Finally! Cara quickened her steps down the marked path and soon arrived at a wooden structure imitating an open box tipped on its side. Its back, cuddled against a hill, was lined with crude bunk beds. With relief she noted a high, chain-link fence stretched across the opening to ensure safety from animals, and a stone fireplace set in a side wall promised cozy warmth. She manipulated the slip latch on the gate and stepped through the fence. Standing inside on the dry concrete floor, she swung the twenty-pound pack from her shoulders with a groan.

As she stretched her arms overhead to relieve the tightness in her back, the drizzle changed to rain. Softly at first, the drops brushed against the corrugated metal roof like a whisk on a snare drum. Suddenly, the skies opened. Water pelting the shelter thrummed like an orchestra of timpani.

She glanced up. Nothing like a little water hitting metal to remind her that sometimes one had to take the bad with the good.

Within minutes Cara organized her provisions. From her pack, she retrieved a camper's stove. After setting some water to boil, she touched a match to the kindling already in the fireplace and added a log from the pile in the corner. Slipping her jacket off, she watched as the blaze leaped against the dark stone. She remembered spending nights like this under nothing more than a tarp on open ground, huddled in an oversized sleeping bag. She would crawl in with her sister, Ellen, and they would share ghost stories and tales of gallant knights and beautiful princesses.

A pang of grief tugged at her.

The water on the stove bubbled and gurgled, pulling her from her memories. Cara poured the hot water over a tea bag set in an aluminum mug, concentrating on the action, keeping the images of the past at bay.

As she sipped hot tea minutes later, her thoughts wandered. The grayness of the clouds reminded her of the walls in her sister's hospital room. She didn't want to remember those last weeks. Ellen's still form on the bed. The sorrowful faces of doctors who had run out of options. Hearing the hospital chaplain's words about God's plan, all the while knowing she might have prevented the collision and her sister's death, if only she had driven that night. If only—

Metal links jangled behind her. Cara whirled to face the fence, yelping as hot tea burned her fingers. In the murky light, she could make out a shadowy figure outside the shelter, fumbling with the gate latch.

A rush of fear chilled her.

After stepping inside, the man shoved the latch back in place and hesitated on the threshold. "Terrific fire you've got here. You don't mind if I share, do you?" His voice, deep and resonant, carried easily over the steady roar of the rain.

She wanted to say, "Yes, I mind. Go find your own fire." But she couldn't. Trail courtesy demanded that anyone caught out in weather like this be given sanctuary. Even a man who could easily overpower her. She collected herself enough to say, "N-no."

Still he hovered at the gate, watchful, clearly unsure of his welcome.

She coughed. "I mean, no problem. Come on in."

He brushed past her toward the heat, his hands outstretched. "Thanks."

Keeping an eye on her unexpected visitor, she edged toward the bunk post where her open pack lay. Inside was her Swiss army knife. Trail courtesy was one thing. Common sense was another. She was alone with a broad-shouldered stranger.

"Where did you hike from?" she asked, keeping her voice casual.

"The trailhead on Route 76."

The same place she had entered yesterday. Cara's fingers fumbled inside the pack until she pulled the knife out. As she slid it into her pocket, she studied her visitor. The flickering light silhouetted a man just a few inches taller than she. Something about the way he held himself seemed vaguely familiar.

"I can't remember the last time I've felt this cold," he continued, his back still toward her. He gathered the bottom of his cable-knit sweater in his hands and twisted. Water streamed to the floor. "Or been this wet." He shifted just enough to talk to her but not enough to deprive his hands of warmth. "The whole time I'm climbing down the hill, I'm wondering, In this wilderness, what are my chances of an ark?"

Her eyebrows rose. "Ark?"

He grinned. "Noah? The Flood?"

She found herself smiling back. "Right. Sorry, no ark."

He shrugged and studied the shelter as if judging its merits. "But we do have a fire. And a roof." He cringed as the downpour intensified. "And sound effects. What more could we ask?"

"Can't think of a thing." She was amazed he was taking the situation so well. Most guys she knew would be complaining furiously.

He faced her. "I do appreciate this."

She nodded, and in a sweeping glance, Cara assessed his hiking boots, jeans, and waist pack. Mud caked everything, and water dripped from his soaked sleeves. Cara moved her gaze up past the sweater, trying to adjust to the presence of this well-muscled, personable, drenched — she froze.

Gorgeous.

A familiar gorgeous. The gorgeous guy she had noticed in the halls at the Silver Pines Resort. He had usually been with a woman. But his face had intrigued her. Even now, with his relaxed expression, she noted how his square jaw reflected an underlying strength of character. His hair — brown as she remembered seeing it in the fluorescent light — was beginning to wave naturally as it dried. In the waning light of the shelter, she could not see the exact color of his eyes, but they held an honest regard that she found attractive.

He should be a model for outdoor gear, Cara thought. He could sell me anything.

"You're with the Doncaster trip, aren't you?" Cara asked.

After a moment's hesitation, he said, "Yes," and shifted a bit closer to the fire.

Cara forced her brain to work. He must be one of the other Doncaster Foundation applicants. Okay, she still didn't know him, but at least she had some assurance he was not a crazed killer. If her own experience in the application review process was any indication, Doncaster accepted only upstanding citizens to receive its grants.

Relieved, Cara gave him a smile and offered her hand. "So am I. I'm Caralyn."

Her fellow applicant produced a winning grin of his own. "Well, what do you know? I didn't think anyone else had ventured away from the resort. I'm Jason."

His hand surrounded hers with firm warmth. Rational thought fled. She wanted to hold on. Hold on to the solid steadiness his grip promised. His questioning gaze told her that he, too, was experiencing something unusual. Connection. Attraction shimmered between them.

He released her to push dripping, dark hair off his forehead.

Cara fought the urge to help him. What was wrong with her?

"So how did your interviews go?" she asked hurriedly, trying to fill in the awkward silence.

"Fine. They went just fine."

He seemed to answer too quickly. Maybe all was not fine. Cara decided it might be a good idea to avoid discussing Doncaster, since they were in competition. Before Cara could find another subject, her companion began to shiver in uncontrollable bursts.

He crossed his arms tightly. "If the troops at Valley Forge with General Washington felt this cold," he said through chattering teeth, "I know why they crossed the Delaware River to take Trenton on Christmas. They probably would have done anything to get to a fire and shelter."

Noah. Washington. Who else will he bring up in conversation tonight? Her instincts took over. The man was freezing. "You should get out of those clothes."

Jason's eyes widened, and he shook again. "Excuse me?"

"The clothes." She took a step toward him, thinking to help with the bulky fabric. "I think you should take them off. Rain and cold add up to lost body heat. You're a prime candidate for hypothermia."

"Oh. Good thinking," he said slowly. "But — uh, my luggage seems to be missing."

"No problem. I can fix that."

Cara rummaged through her pack and fished out one pullover hoody, a nylon zippered rain jacket, sweatpants, and a pair of woolen socks. For hiking she bought her clothes in comfortable large sizes, so she guessed these would fit him. She also found her hooded, all-weather blanket and handed everything to him.

"Here, put these on. Then wrap yourself in the blanket and sit close to the fire." To ease the wariness she still sensed in him, she added brightly, "And don't worry, I don't take advantage of strange men."

"How about normal ones?" His lopsided grin caused Cara a tingle of enjoyment.

"Not when they're freezing."

He shivered again and moved to the corner farthest from the fireplace.

Turning her back, Cara took a deep breath. His smile sure packed a wallop. She'd do well to remember he *was* a stranger.

Good-looking. Funny. But a complete stranger. She pulled a length of lightweight rope from her pack and strung a line from a nail in one wall to the corner post of the bunk beds, keeping her back toward him. If they were to spend some time together, she had better learn a little more about him.

"So what's the deal with General Washington? He's not the most common subject for name-dropping."

"I got my undergraduate degree in American history..." His words were muffled, almost lost behind cloth, then became clear. "And I never lost the fascination."

"American history, hmm?" She tied the last knot in the rope. "Let me see how much I remember. 1776, the Revolutionary War. 1861, the Civil War." Behind her, wet cloth slapped on the concrete. She ignored it. "1929, the Wall Street crash. 1966, the Topeka Tornado—"

"The Topeka Tornado?" Jason broke in. "I think I missed something. This was a *major* event in the history of the United States?"

"It was for the people in Topeka. The dome of the state capital was damaged. Sections of town were flattened—"

He gave a laughing protest. "Okay, I believe you. Starting now, I'm adding the Topeka Tornado to my list of major twentieth century events."

Grinning, Cara retrieved Jason's garments and gently squeezed the cloth outside the slightly opened gate, letting the water drip in the area protected by the overhanging roof. From the corner, she heard more rustling cloth.

"Kansas Jayhawks?" he said. "Are you from the University of Kansas?"

Cara glanced his way to find him staring at the plump bird emblazoned on the black sweatshirt he now wore. The overlarge yellow beak, blue feathers, and ridiculous grin marched across the material in wild abandon.

"Yes, actually. I work there." She moved to hang the clothes carefully on the line.

"I've always thought," Jason said, "that the Jayhawk was created by a student who indulged in alcohol to excess. I guess you could say he's cute... in an obnoxious sort of way."

Cara faced him. "Did you go to KU?"

He shook his head. "No, but I've got a friend who teaches there." He reached for her rain jacket. "What do you do at the university?"

"I'm a reference librarian at the main library."

"Ah, the noble calling of librarian." At her skeptical glance, he chuckled. "No, I'm serious. A great librarian saved my hide a couple of times when I was working on my history degree. I have a lot of respect for what you do."

Cara glowed inside and her lips curved up. "Thanks. People don't always appreciate our work. The *old-lady-with-the-bun* image gets in the way."

"Although you're a lady," he teased, "you're definitely not old, and I don't see a bun. I think we can safely put the cliché to rest."

Cara blushed. His voice was light, but she could feel his eyes on her.

He was feeling less like a stranger by the minute.

Jason pulled on the jacket, held the tab of the zipper a moment, and then dropped it to leave the jacket open. "So. Are you originally from Kansas?"

"No, Pennsylvania. But I've come to love it here in the Land of Oz," she answered then waited for the inevitable teasing. She prompted, "Well?"

"Oh no," he said with a grin. "I will *not* say a word about Dorothy or Toto. I tried an Oz joke on Nate once — my friend at KU — and it almost ended the friendship."

Laughing lightly, she changed the subject. "So, I've taught you about the Topeka Tornado. Tell me about where you're from."

Jason stuffed his hands in his pockets and regarded the ceiling beams. "Well, let's see," he said slowly. "I grew up in Washington D.C. Natural disasters are more likely to come in the form of political upheaval with a little violent crime thrown in. If you believe the news."

"And you don't?" Cara moved outside the fence to scoop more water from the rain barrel.

He sat near the fire, his back against one of the bunk posts. "I didn't see much crime personally. Washington is a city of action, of change. A city can't replace an entire section of its population every four years without stress. There's always tension in the air. An underlying message, like *Gotta hurry, we don't have much time*."

As Jason spoke, Cara added water to the pot on the stove, then sank down on the bottom bunk facing him. It was easier to hear him now. The rain had subsided, a gentle patter replaced the deafening roof thunder.

His voice and manner captivated her. He talked about riding the crowded and efficient D.C. subway to see the national monuments. Walking through the Smithsonian Air and Space Museum to gaze at vintage aircraft hanging overhead. Theaters where dignitaries and royalty were as likely to show up as college professors. Ethnic restaurants tucked away on tree-lined streets. Traffic circles invented specifically to confuse tourists. He brought everything alive with vivid descriptions. A born storyteller.

He had wrapped the blanket completely around himself and was leaning back on the post, the flickering light playing over his handsome face. She let out a slow, even breath.

She had come up to the mountain for solitude and some quiet time, but she was glad Jason had happened along. She enjoyed his company... and found herself hoping she could see him again after tonight.

That thought brought her up short. She had just met the man. They were in competition for grant money. Seeing him again would be impossible.

"I was fortunate," he was saying. "I saw a lot of Washington's good side."

"So, how do you like the Midwest?" she asked.

"It's... different."

"Spoken like a true Easterner." Cara laughed and shook her head. "Let me guess. Slower, more rural, we're fascinated by weather and agriculture. In Lawrence, things are a little more cosmopolitan because of the university, but it still took me six months to adjust. Once I got over the shock? I don't think I could live anywhere else." She noticed his indulgent smile and his slight shiver. "Hey, you're still cold. Let me get you something warm to drink."

She got up and dropped a teabag into the saucepan heating on the stove, all the while conscious of him observing her. After squeezing a foil packet of honey into the tea, she held the pan out to him by the handle.

"Sorry, I had only one cup with me. Earl Grey with honey," she said. "It's not fancy, but it is hot. I hope it's not too strong."

He glanced up, and Cara studied his face. Exposure to the elements had taken its toll. His pasty color worried her, but his hair was drying, and once he got the hot drink down, he'd be warm inside. Just like his friendly expression now warmed her.

"It'll be wonderful," he said. "I feel cold all the way to my bones."

He took the pan by the handle, his fingers curling over hers as he sought a good hold. A burst of distant lightning outside the shelter mirrored the sensation springing up Cara's arm. Her first reaction was to jerk away. Gentle pressure from his hand stopped her and probably saved him from getting burned. He placed a second hand on the handle to steady the pot, all the while searching her face as if looking for an answer only she held. She slowly, carefully disentangled her hand.

Where was this feeling coming from? She'd met good--looking men before. Even dated a few. Yet she had never known this... anticipation, this certainty that something bigger, more exciting, could be hers — with him. The unfamiliar feeling scared her and drew her in.

Thankfully Jason interrupted her reverie. "Mm, hot," he muttered after he sipped from the pot. "This is great." He paused. "You know, the smell of the fire reminds me of Boy Scout camp. S'mores with oozing marshmallows, songs around the campfire..."

"I thought Boy Scouts were always prepared," Cara teased, grateful for the return to light conversation.

To her surprise, he laughed in agreement. "This Boy Scout wouldn't earn any badges for this little stunt. It was plain stupid to hike up here without checking the weather or grabbing my jacket. I won't make that mistake again."

His honesty touched a responsive chord in her. "Glad to hear it."

They both fell silent. Instead of metallic roof patter, Cara could now hear dripping from the firs and pines and a soft stirring of the wind through the trees. The fire snapped in front of her.

Jason began softly humming a slow tune. Cara immediately recognized an African folk song she had learned at summer camp. As she sat on the edge of the lower bunk, she joined in, her alto blending easily with his tenor. On the next verse, Jason added the words.

"*Kumbaya, my Lord. Kumbaya.*" Together they hummed and sang, each remembering verses the other didn't. They ended on a soft note.

"Do you know what the words mean?" Cara asked.

"*Come by here, my Lord* was what a camp counselor told me."

A prayer. From his reverent manner, she knew Jason had sung the song as a prayer. She wondered if he thought he would get an answer.

Cara sank down beside him, thinking to change the atmosphere. She drew her jacket close and started singing "Row, Row, Row Your Boat."

After a few false starts to find an acceptable key, they were singing the round with gusto. The last refrain echoed into the night. They laughed loud and long. Cara couldn't remember the last time she had felt so comfortable and energized.

Between gasps, she said, "If there are other hikers within twenty miles of us, they're probably cursing their luck to be serenaded by two makeshift opera stars."

"You have a great voice, but our duet had a certain—" He paused to look out into the night sky. "Is the moon out tonight? I'd hate to be mistaken for a wolf."

Cara checked her watch with an exaggerated gesture, and a smile lightened her voice. "By my calculations, the moon was up an hour ago."

"Too late. Wonder what the penalty is for impersonating wildlife?"

"Going through more interviews for Doncaster."

"Right," he said and chuckled.

An unassuming guy who liked to sing and had a great sense of humor. *A kindred spirit.* After losing her sister, she had wondered if she would ever meet someone with whom she would feel this close, this connected. A hushed peace settled within Cara. She threw another log on the fire, completely at ease with the company and her surroundings.

"So, what line of charity are you in?" Jason said.

His unexpected question caught her by surprise. Even though she had joked about Doncaster just now, she didn't want to talk about it. Especially when things were going so well between them. She decided to give him only the bare bones description.

"I've established a research fund specifically for closed-head injury. To help doctors treating victims of head trauma. And to support prevention efforts."

"Sounds like a good idea. And what have you done so far?" Jason asked the question with the manner of a serious businessman.

Proud of her work, Cara answered more freely. "We're in our third year. We've been able to fund a few small research projects in Wichita and Topeka, but I'm hoping to expand. I've retained the services of an attorney and a financial planner to map out a strategy for the next few years. We have non-profit status, and we're setting up interest-earning trust funds. And, of course, I applied to Doncaster about four months ago."

Jason nodded in acknowledgment. "If you made it this far through the process, you've done your homework."

"Yes, I have." Approaching charity as a business, she was learning, swayed contributors as much as pointing out the benefits to the recipients. "What about you? What kind of charity are you working on?"

He cleared his throat. "I... uh, I haven't actually applied to Doncaster."

"Oh?" she said in confusion.

"I'm from the home office in Washington D.C." He faced her and spoke lightly. "In fact, I'm Jason Montague, Doncaster's Chairman of the Board."

End of Excerpt

The Master's Plan **by LaVerne St. George**

Available as an E-book and in paperback

About the Author

First there were crayon drawings in grade school, then books of space travel, mysteries and espionage. I've always carried stories in my head and written them down. In college, my aunt sent me a box of books, including Kathleen Woodiwiss' *The Flame and the Flower*. I caught romance fever and never looked back. Now with several books and awards to my credit, I continue to write and promote books that lift the Spirit.

When I'm not writing, I enjoy crocheting, bird watching, traveling, and jigsaw puzzles. I'm an avid fan of romance in all its variety, and my favorite diversion is a well-written book with a happy ending. Thank you for reading *Just Ducky*.

Connect With LaVerne

On social media, you can find me on Facebook, Instagram, Pinterest, and Goodreads.

Visit my website, **www.LStGeorge.com**, for news and my Blog: Writing in the Spirit.

Sign up for the Sweet Times Newsletter

www.LStGeorge.com/Sweet-Times

Sweet Contemporary Romance by LaVerne St. George

A Love He Can Trust. **Pittsburgh Connections, Book 1.**

Available in print and eBook.

"Never date an employee."

That's David Mansfield's personal rule, and he's sticking to it. Hayley Lancaster knows that getting involved with someone at work is a risky proposition.

Past betrayals make David cautious; he'd like to let down his guard. If only she didn't work in his company. If only she wasn't dating his former friend, now arch rival. It doesn't take long for Hayley to realize that against her better judgment, she's falling for the boss. When David's interest suddenly cools, Hayley is devastated. She expects to lose her job—she just wishes she hadn't lost her heart.

~~

Carousel Magic. **Pittsburgh Connections, Book 2.**

Novelette. Available in print and eBook.

Thomas Martin never lets feelings get in the way of doing business. As the new owner of the local amusement park, he's determined to replace the old carousel with video games. The town's mayor, Ginger Fairchild, is equally determined to save the vintage carousel from the bulldozer. The park needs a lot of work before opening day. There's not much time. Can Ginger persuade Tom of the carousel's value before it's too late? Does the carousel have enough magic left to change just two more hearts?

Also published in the Sweet Romance Anthology: *Autumn's Kiss*. From Open Book Romances. Available until Feb. 28, 2025 as eBook.

Looking for more Sweet Romance? Try this novella anthology! Eight sweet stories of love. Eight great authors. Eight ways to celebrate autumn.

Falling in love is timeless. From a sexy medieval stonemason to a big-time businessman — Regency England to Napa Vineyards — this selection of Historical, Contemporary, Paranormal and Time-Travel romance novellas is sure to capture your heart.

~~

Restore My Heart. **Pittsburgh Connections, Book 3.**

Available in print and eBook.

Sally Myers is no fan of the holidays or of working-class men who don't fit into her new life as a college-educated professional. Enter Jefferson Campbell, a master craftsman who arrives in town to restore the vintage carousel. Sally wants no part of Jeff's "hands-on" approach, and the fact that he'll soon be leaving for another restoration job earns Jeff no points. But the "carousel man" is smitten and makes a holiday wish – that he'll grab the brass ring and win Sally's heart.

~~

Visit My Website: **www.LStGeorge.com**

Contemporary Inspirational Romance by LaVerne St. George

Just Ducky.

Available as an eBook and in print.

~Love may require breaking someone's heart. Even your own~

After the death of her father, librarian Marian Fletcher wraps herself in a protective net of quiet control, few social gatherings, and routine. When Gill Gillespie, her high school crush, shows up as her new neighbor and then as her partner on an important work project, he helps Marian awaken to a larger life as well as to love. However, Gill is caught in a net of his own, bound by family expectations and a childhood girlfriend, a net he fails to see until it threatens his chances with the woman who has captured his heart.

~~

The Master's Plan.

Available as eBook and in print.

For Caralyn Masters, an accident leaves lingering effects — she grieves for her sister and automobiles give her the literal shakes. She focuses on her job as a university librarian and on creating a charitable fund to support closed-head trauma research, but money is tight. While hiking in the Ozarks, she shares a trail shelter with a wet and weary hiker. He's charming. She's attracted. Things are looking up.

Jason Montague counts his blessings. His unplanned hike ended in the company of an experienced hiker. He's captivated by Cara, but as the Doncaster Foundation's chairman, he holds the future of her charity in his hands. When he's forced to reveal his epilepsy, his hope for a personal relationship vanishes. Back at Doncaster's Midwest office, Jason discovers missing money, a missing employee, and negative media spin. Things are not looking good.

~Bad Things Happen. Then Love Steps In.~

Visit My Website: **www.LStGeorge.com**

www.ingramcontent.com/pod-product-compliance
Lightning Source LLC
Chambersburg PA
CBHW071257130626
46556CB00003B/1354